WORD POWER
QUIZ

WORD POWER QUIZ

SUJATA RAY

RUPA

Published by
Rupa Publications India Pvt. Ltd 1991
7/16, Ansari Road, Daryaganj
New Delhi 110 002

Sales Centres:

Allahabad Bengaluru Chennai
Hyderabad Jaipur Kathmandu
Kolkata Mumbai

ISBN: 978-81-716-7057-4

Seventh impression 2019

10 9 8 7

This book is dedicated to
the first modern lexicographer,
who called himself a harmless drudge

This is not a quiz book to test whether you know the meaning of palimpsest or eelymosynary, words you would very rarely use or rarely come across. The 1000 words on which the quizzes have been set are words one comes across in reading, although at an advanced level, and writing, in any but bureaucratese. A person who can use words precisely doesn't use the wrong word or fumble for the exact meaning, has acquired a formidable power called wordpower, which communicates, convinces, and conquers. If reading or writing is your business, you must master words.

No learning is more effective than learning through mistakes. In the quizzes that follow the choices are very close; they take care of the mistakes we make from the sound of a word, their similarity with other words, their seeming connection with familiar root words or prefixes and suffixes. A dictionary doesn't allow you to make mistakes; you find the meaning with very little effort; and what is effortlessly learnt may be soon forgotten. Try any ten quizzes, and you may find that you need to know more precisely, and to attach exact meanings to words you come across or use.

The synonym section of the quizzes is the most important. Once you know the *exact* meaning, finding the antonym is not difficult. The trouble is, many words have more than one meaning, or more than one application, depending on the context. It is the identification of the context that is the crucial test of the antonym quizzes.

And spellings, well they are every educated English speaker's nightmare, including the native speakers. If one is mortified when one discovers a mistake one has been habitually making, it is a good sign; the mortification is some assurance that one takes spellings seriously.

There are some quizzes on loan words in English. Not only is the discovery that a word we always thought of as pucca, is in fact an old borrowing or a new introduction, the point is that if such a powerful language as English can live happily with so many loan words, why can't we? Accepting words from other languages is not a sign of poverty, but strength, great strength in fact.

Vocabulary tests are now widespread; in most competitive tests they are an important item. The reason is simple; a person's command of vocabulary is a proof of their reading, and the higher the level of attentive reading, the stronger it is. There is simply no other way of acquiring a strong word sense but by reading more, and yet more.

One word of caution about word quizzes. One should take them in small doses; not too many words at once, or else much will escape your memory.

New Delhi
April 1991   **S R**

CONTENTS

I
WHAT DOES IT REALLY MEAN?

In this section, justifiably the longest, each headword is followed by five possible choices, out of which only one is correct. The others sound possible, because either the headword has triggered off the memory of similar-sounding words, or one element of it is masquerading as a root. These headwords are very commonly used, and quite often not exactly rightly, although the meaning may come close enough. A word is used to convey a *particular* idea, and it is important to get that particular meaning. The more serious reading you do, the more important it is to know what exactly is being said, and similarly, when you are writing seriously, you need the only possible word that will convey what you are saying.

Words often have more than one meaning; it is not always that in these quizzes you will be offered the most common. Your task is to eliminate the wrong choices, and pick out the one that corresponds to the headword.

1. INTERNECINE: (a) internal (b) continuous (c) bloody (d) international (e) mutually destructive
2. SLEAZY: (a) dirty (b) cheap (c) smelly (d) disreputable (e) malodorous
3. INANE: (a) injudicious (b) hostile (c) insensitive (d) crude (e) senseless
4. TERMAGANT: (a) poisonous (b) sour (c) very hot (d) harlot (e) shrew
5. EXACERBATE: (a) aggravate (b) mediate (c) impose strictness (d) exaggerate (e) eliminate
6. MANIFEST: (a) obvious (b) prominent (c) popular (d) unchangeable (d) certain

1. (e)
2. (d)
3. (e)
4. (e)
5. (a)
6. (a)

7. INCRIMINATE: (a) involve (b) suggest (c) accuse (d) abuse (e) excuse oneself
8. NOISOME: (a) loud (b) boisterous (c) brawling (d) foul smelling (e) dirty
9. ESCHEW: (a) swallow (b) shun (c) surrender (d) digest (e) violate
10. DOLOROUS: (a) musical (b) noisy (c) mournful (d) languorous (e) lazy
11. CADAVEROUS: (a) ugly (b) fierce-looking (c) pale (d) ghostly (e) frightening
12. TACITURN: (a) uncommunicative (b) ill-tempered (c) ungenerous (d) unfriendly (e) unwilling to oblige
13. INSIPID: (a) bland (b) harmless (c) rotten (d) colourless (e) vulgar
14. GINGERLY: (a) sharply (b) inimical (c) very carefully (d) very fast (e) offensively insulting
15. MATRIX: (a) standard (b) format (c) measure (d) mould (e) proforma
16. INTRACTABLE: (a) immeasurable (b) refractory (c) insurmountable (d) untraceable (e) difficult
17. HISTRIONIC: (a) theatrical (b) hysterical (c) historical (d) sensational (e) magical
18. CONUNDRUM: (a) subtle argument (b) riddle (c) myth (d) grinding agent (e) a mineral
19. BRACKISH: (a) dirty (b) muddy (c) stale (d) salty (e) smelly
20. TRADUCE: (a) violate (b) calumniate (c) breach (d) transgress (e) seduce
21. YAHOO: (a) the vulgar rich (b) the *nouveaux riches* (c) uncultivated person (d) brute in human shape (e) a foreigner
22. HIERARCHY: (a) aristocracy (b) upper echelons (c) power structure (d) gradation (e) degrees of nobility
23. ARCANE: (a) difficult (b) obscure (c) mysterious (d) obscene (e) pedantic

7. (c)
8. (d)
9. (b)
10. (c)
11. (c)
12. (a)
13. (a)
14. (c)
15. (d)
16. (b)
17. (a)
18. (b)
19. (d)
20. (b)
21. (d)
22. (d)
23. (c)

24. TRUMPERY: (a) fabrication (b) deception (c) worthless finery (d) trumpet call (e) tidbits
25. STULTIFY: (a) impair (b) block (c) destroy (d) stop progress (e) sabotage
26. BELLICOSE: (a) inimical (b) full of hatred (c) warlike (d) with a bulging stomach (e) harmful
27. SECULAR: (a) spectacular (b) religious (c) secure (d) material (e) temporal
28. INVEIGLE: (a) cajole (b) instigate (c) condemn (d) expose (e) cancel
29. PARADIGM: (a) parable (b) parapet (c) particularity (d) pattern (e) partial
30. MEGALOMANIA: (a) excessive preoccupation with wealth (b) love for unlimited power (c) delusions of grandeur (d) craving for immortality (e) superiority complex
31. SEDENTARY: (a) requiring the use of brain (b) clerical (c) sleepy (d) requiring sitting (e) staid
32. INSCRUTABLE: (a) difficult (b) enigmatic (c) unpredictable (d) obscure (e) mysterious
33. TORPID: (a) hot (b) turbulent (c) dull (d) stormy (e) steamy
34. FRET: (a) worry (b) behave impatiently (c) pine (d) regret (e) complain
35. VACUOUS: (a) vacant (b) insubstantial (c) vague (d) inane (e) meaningless
36. BLASÉ : (a) bored (b) self-satisfied (c) ignorant (d) all-knowing (e) perverted
37. THRALDOM: (a) state of enslavement (b) state of enchantment (c) state of benumbment (d) state of subjugation (e) trance
38. MAUDLIN: (a) sentimental (b) commonplace (c) insincere (d) false (e) embarrassing
39. EXCORIATE: (a) worsen (b) resolve (c) complicate (d) flay (e) fleece

24. (c)
25. (a)
26. (c)
27. (e)
28. (a)
29. (d)
30. (c)
31. (d)
32. (b)
33. (c)
34. (a)
35. (d)
36. (a)
37. (a)
38. (a)
39. (d)

40. SIBLING: (a) baby at the breast (b) relative (c) blood relation (d) brother or sister (e) step-brother
41. EXPLOIT: (a) an affair with a woman (b) expedition (c) heroic deed (d) magical feat (e) performance of an impossible task
42. EXPURGATE: (a) expel (b) purge (c) improve (d) remove offensive matter (e) purify
43. DOWDY: (a) vulgar (b) overdressed (c) shabby (d) whorish (e) queer
44. VAUNTING: (a) jumping over (b) displaying (c) boasting (d) overwhelming (e) defying
45. MASOCHIST: (a) one who indulges in abnormal sexual practices (b) a woman paid to whip her client (c) one who derives pleasure from pain (d) one who derives pleasure from giving others pain (e) an introverted person
46. ZANY: (a) bizarre (b) buffoon (c) demented (d) funny (e) outlandish
47. RETRACTION: (a) confession (b) perverseness (c) diversion (d) withdrawal (e) affirmation
48. SIMPERING: (a) pretending to cry (b) smiling in a silly self-conscious manner (c) making servile praise (d) behaving in a humble and oily manner (e) uttering gibberish
49. CONTUMACY: (a) illwill (b) stubbornness (c) anger (d) insubordination (e) contempt
50. RETICENCE: (a) rectitude (b) taciturnity (c) reluctance (d) refusal (e) unwillingness
51. SATIATED: (a) persuaded (b) completed (c) convinced (d) spirited (e) surfeited
52. PRISTINE: (a) pure (b) unspoilt (c) original (d) holy (e) natural
53. ACERBIC: (a) sour (b) foul (c) undecided (d) quarrelsome (e) strong
54. TANTALIZING: (a) setting an unattainable target (b) scandalous (c) fascinating (d) tormenting (e) enthralling

40. (d)
41. (c)
42. (d)
43. (c)
44. (c)
45. (c)
46. (d)
47. (d)
48. (b)
49. (d)
50. (b)
51. (e)
52. (b)
53. (a)
54. (d)

55. RECALCITRANT: (a) refractory (b) unwilling (c) contrite (d) contrary (e) hesitant
56. ACQUIESCE: (a) accept (b) acknowledge (c) acquire (d) refuse (e) accommodate
57. PERPETRATE: (a) perpetuate a wrong (b) commit an offence (c) perform an atrocity (d) sanction a wrong (e) pardon an offence
58. BERATE: (a) urge (b) encourage (c) beat up (d) severely scold (e) underrate
59. REPARATION: (a) amendment (b) compensation (c) making truce (d) making up (e) negotiation
60. SHIBBOLETH: (a) superstition (b) test word (c) antiquated custom (d) mumbo jumbo (e) tenets of faith
61. EXIGENCY: (a) instability (b) emergency (c) state of war (d) excessive expenditure (e) waste
62. PROPHYLACTIC: (a) germ-killing (b) curative (c) cleansing (d) disease preventing (e) anti-viral
63. ACRIMONIOUS: (a) tearful (b) loud (c) pathetic (d) caustic (e) prolonged
64. CANKER: (a) thorn (b) obstacle (c) evil that spreads (d) cancerous growth (e) dirt that clings
65. SPAWN: (a) breed (b) lay eggs (c) proliferate (d) warm up (e) spread out
66. DURESS: (a) pressure (b) extortion (c) prowess (d) subjugation (e) unlawful restraint
67. SOBRIQUET: (a) honorific title (b) brickbat (c) praise (d) testimonial (e) nickname
68. DYNAMIC: (a) charged with electrical energy (b) passionate (c) explosive (d) forceful (e) impatient
69. RIBALD: (a) coarse (b) loud (c) irreverent (d) sarcastic (e) angry
70. ECCENTRIC: (a) unreasonable (b) perverse (c) whimsical (d) quick (e) peripatetic

55. (a)
56. (a)
57. (b)
58. (d)
59. (b)
60. (b)
61. (b)
62. (d)
63. (d)
64. (c)
65. (b)
66. (e)
67. (e)
68. (d)
69. (a)
70. (c)

71. CANTANKEROUS: (a) loudly complaining (b) angry (c) fault-finding (d) quarrelsome (e) nasty
72. RANCOUR: (a) bad odour (b) grievance (c) richness (d) spite (e) noise
73. PROPITIATE: (a) satisfy (b) amend (c) compensate (d) delay (e) appease
74. CAPTIOUS: (a) capable (b) spacious (c) courageous (d) imprisoned (e) fault-finding
75. RENEGE: (a) withdraw (b) desert (c) deny (d) go back on (e) repent
76. PRODIGAL: (a) highly talented (b) repentant (c) generous (d) recklessly wasteful (e) stingy
77. AEGIS: (a) banner (b) jurisdiction (c) period (d) protection (e) patronage
78. CONCEIT: (a) arrogance (b) false argument (c) wrong notion (d) deception (e) fanciful idea
79. SATURNINE: (a) wise (b) unstable (c) ancient (d) gloomy (e) sour
80. EPHEMERAL: (a) temporary (b) vague (c) of light interest (d) shortlived (e) heavenly
81. TRUCULENT: (a) reluctant (b) hesitant (c) unwilling (d) aggressive (e) reserved
82. DISCURSIVE: (a) rambling (b) topics to be discussed (c) miscellaneous (d) instructive (e) difficult
83. PERSIFLAGE: (a) exchange of insults (b) rude comments (c) rubbish (d) tall talk (e) frivolity
84. RETROGRADE: (a) reprehensible (b) revolutionary (c) divisive (d) going backward (e) reactionary
85. DERELICT: (a) broken down (b) abandoned (c) haunted (d) empty (e) ruined
86. YEN: (a) love (b) passion (c) longing (d) sympathy (e) attraction
87. TERRESTRIAL: (a) skyey (b) cosmic (c) earthly (d) of the solar system (e) of the soil

71. (d)
72. (d)
73. (e)
74. (e)
75. (d)
76. (d)
77. (d)
78. (e)
79. (d)
80. (d)
81. (d)
82. (a)
83. (e)
84. (d)
85. (b)
86. (c)
87. (c)

88. APOTHEOSIS: (a) development (b) resolution (c) decomposition (d) deification (e) change
89. UNCTUOUS: (a) servile (b) insidious (c) evil (d) greasy (e) assuming a mask of holiness
90. NEFARIOUS: (a) illegal (b) criminal (c) wicked (d) surreptitious (e) conspiratorial
91. MISCEGENATION (pronounced 'misigination'): (a) mixing wrongly (b) wrong experimentation (c) interbreeding between races (d) mismatching of genes (e) marriage between incompatible partners
92. CONGENITAL: (a) pleasant (b) favourable (c) of the penis (d) existing at birth (e) inducing a happy frame of mind
93. RAREFIED: (a) scarce (b) thinned out (c) antique (d) seldom (e) rasping
94. SULTRY: (a) humid (b) hot (c) hot and humid (d) dry and hot (e) desiccating
95. AFFABLE: (a) smiling (b) courtly (c) helpful (d) haughty (e) friendly
96. NEMESIS: (a) repentance (b) regret (c) forgiveness (d) agent of revenge (e) scales of justice
97. EPICUREAN: (a) one who follows the path of strict morality (b) an impassive person (c) hedonistic (d) one who believes in a system of values (e) one who does not believe in an afterworld
98. SCHISM: (a) controversy (b) split (c) infighting (d) divisiveness (e) separation
99. NEXUS: (a) bond (b) chain (c) order (d) evil-smelling (e) connection
100. SUBTERFUGE: (a) safe shelter (b) evasion (c) resorting to excuse (d) cunning (e) pretence
101. SUCCINCT: (a) exact (b) correct (c) brief (d) terse (e) meaningful

88. (d)
89. (d)
90. (c)
91. (c)
92. (d)
93. (b)
94. (c)
95. (e)
96. (d)
97. (c)
98. (b)
99. (e)
100. (b)
101. (e)

102. AMBIDEXTROUS: (a) one who can use either hand with skill (b) one who is skilled in many things (c) a person with only one hand (d) one whose skill is in doubt (e) a supremely skilled person

103. GULLIBLE: (a) stupid (b) accountable (c) easily swallowed (d) easily deceived (e) possible

104. INDICT (pronounced 'in dait'): (a) convict (b) compose (c) point out (d) charge (e) arrest

105. SCINTILLATE: (a) simmer (b) seethe (c) ripple (d) sparkle (e) waver

106. DISGRUNTLED: (a) dispirited (b) dejected (c) angry (d) dissatisfied (e) disappointed

107. APHASIA: (a) loss of memory (b) loss of optical lens (c) languor (d) clear memory of a previous life (e) loss of speech

108. SINUOUS: (a) lithe (b) rippling (c) sensuous (d) complicated (e) suggestive

109. EXPOSTULATE: (a) explain at length (b) urge (c) reason (d) prohibit (e) request fervently

110. TRYST: (a) encounter (b) appointment (c) secret meeting place (d) faith between lovers (e) knightly combat

111. VENAL: (a) sinful (b) lustful (c) pardonable (d) corruptible (e) amenable to persuasion

112. MUGWUMP: (a) an independent (b) defector (c) fence-sitter (d) cad (e) corrupt politician

113. INFERNAL: (a) hellish (b) terrible (c) aggravating (d) rowdy (e) fiery

114. TRENCHANT: (a) penetrating (b) savage (c) caustic (d) merciless (e) powerful

115. CONDUCIVE: (a) contributive (b) clinching (c) corroborative (d) contradictory (e) persuasive

116. SNIVEL: (a) cry abjectly (b) whine (c) grovel (d) smirk (e) sneeze

102. (a)
103. (d)
104. (d)
105. (d)
106. (d)
107. (e)
108. (a)
109. (c)
110. (b)
111. (d)
112. (a)
113. (a)
114. (a)
115. (a)
116. (b)

117. APHORISM: (a) a much used phrase (b) a meaningless phrase (c) repetition (d) maxim (e) a vague expression
118. SCOFF: (a) mock (b) condemn (c) reject (d) decry (e) dismiss
119. INDIGENT: (a) native (b) unintelligent (c) bad (d) unfavourable (e) poor
120. SCOURGE: (a) persecute (b) condemn (c) flog (d) decimate (e) destroy
121. CONCOMITANT: (a) that which logically follows (b) in reply (c) pledged (d) accompanying (e) subordinate
122. MARTINET: (a) marital (b) strict parent (c) military (d) strict disciplinarian (e) inhabitant of Mars
123. SUBLIMINAL: (a) most exalted (b) elevating (c) mind below the level of full consciousness but able to influence actions (d) libidinal (e) below the threshold of consciousness
124. TIRADE: (a) denunciation (b) violent speech (c) sustained abuse (d) turbulence of the sea (e) long speech of censure
125. ATROPHY: (a) to stiffen (b) to waste away (c) to change form (d) to hibernate (e) to rot away
126. SUBTLETY: (a) cunning (b) guile (c) deception (d) fine distinction (e) refinement -
127. TOPOGRAPHY: (a) physical features (b) tactical location (c) quality of the soil (d) quantum of fertility (e) geographical location
128. PALL: (a) fade (b) lose interest (c) lose lustre (d) lose appetite (e) become boring
129. BURGEON: (a) batter (b) strengthen (c) bolster (d) flourish (e) encumber
130. OBSEQUIOUS: (a) condoling (b) obscure (c) tough (d) servile (e) helpful
131. TURGID: (a) bombastic (b) unclear (c) turbulent (d) confused (e) very hot

117. (d)
118. (a)
119. (e)
120. (c)
121. (d)
122. (d)
123. (e)
124. (e)
125. (b)
126. (d)
127. (a)
128. (e)
129. (d)
130. (d)
131. (a)

132. **MURKY:** (a) dark (b) questionable (c) conspiratorial (d) shady (e) illegal
133. **ARCHIVES** (pronounced 'ar-kives'): (a) underground vaults (b) library (c) storeroom (d) repository of public records (e) monastic cells
134. **SLEIGHT:** (a) stealth (b) speedy movement (c) dexterity (d) littleness (e) ignoring
135. **SURROGATE:** (a) alternative (b) substitute (c) impostor (d) illegal (e) secret
136. **GIMMICK** ('g' pronounced as in 'give'): (a) lure (b) laborious device (c) magic (d) clever money-making device (e) clever publicity device
137. **SEQUESTERED:** (a) commandeered (b) confiscated (c) set aside (d) secluded (e) cornered
138. **THROES:** (a) anguish (b) bondage (c) overwhelming power (d) spasm (e) leash
139. **CONDIGN:** (a) excessive (b) appropriate (c) mild (d) unjustified (e) merciful
140. **PANACEA:** (a) solution to all problems (b) medicine (c) magical remedy (d) talisman (e) cure-all
141. **SUPPLICATE:** (a) beg favours (b) request earnestly (c) petition humbly (d) repeatedly insist (e) pray for mercy
142. **AMBIENCE:** (a) pleasing surroundings (b) scope (c) atmosphere (d) vastness (e) civilized surroundings
143. **PALLIATE:** (a) become pale (b) ease pain (c) satiate (d) cure (e) emulsify
144. **AMBIVALENT:** (a) a person who has no doubts in his mind (b) decisive (c) hesitant (d) vague (e) with conflicting emotions
145. **SKULK:** (a) resent working (b) brood silently (c) move stealthily (d) shirk work (e) move clumsily

132. (a)
133. (d)
134. (c)
135. (b)
136. (e)
137. (d)
138. (a)
139. (b)
140. (e)
141. (c)
142. (c)
143. (b)
144. (e)
145. (c)

146. MUTABLE: (a) silent (b) changeable (c) transferable (d) that which can be commuted (e) that which can die
147. DEMOTIC: (a) corrupt (b) outlandish (c) debased (d) popular (e) aristocratic
148. TRIBULATION: (a) effort (b) suffering (c) struggle (d) trouble (e) trial
149. NADIR: (a) noisy spot (b) highest point (c) lowest point (d) faraway place (e) epitome
150. DELETERIOUS: (a) harmful (b) delightful (c) corrupting (d) slow (e) encouraging
151. FRUGAL: (a) thrifty (b) healthy (c) bare (d) miserly (e) extravagant
152. BICKER: (a) fight (b) quarrel (c) argue (d) insult (e) delay
153. INCHOATE: (a) rudimentary (b) confused (c) solid (d) inseparable (e) indistinguishable
154. CHARISMA (pronounced 'karisma'): (a) manliness (b) sexual appeal (c) extraordinarily good looks (d) great popular appeal (e) spirituality
155. UNCOUTH: (a) ugly (b) boorish (c) savage (d) ignorant (e) raw
156. ENIGMATIC: (a) strange (b) doubtful (c) meaningful (d) full of wisdom (e) puzzling
157. INCIPIENT: (a) confused (b) chaotic (c) open (d) outrageous (e) beginning
158. FOREBODING: (a) fear (b) prediction of disaster (c) feeling of impending disaster (d) courage in the face of adversity (e) prohibition
159. DERIDE: (a) accuse (b) ridicule (c) dismiss (d) criticise (e) treat with contempt
160. PERJURY: (a) treachery (b) bearing false witness (c) conspiracy (d) larceny (e) lying under oath
161. IMPETUOUS: (a) impatient (b) impulsive (c) emotional (d) thoughtless (e) inconsiderate

146. (b)
147. (d)
148. (b)
149. (c)
150. (a)
151. (a)
152. (b)
153. (a)
154. (d)
155. (b)
156. (e)
157. (e)
158. (c)
159. (b)
160. (e)
161. (b)

162. CLIMACTIC: (a) menopause (b) concerning the weather (c) of the highest point (d) anti-climax (e) cataclysmic
163. HAPLESS: (a) unfortunate (b) helpless (c) desperate (d) incident-free (e) turbulent
164. CREDULITY: (a) credibility (b) disbelief (c) suspicion (d) rational approach (e) eagerness to believe
165. TRACTABLE: (a) traceable (b) cultivable (c) docile (d) friendly (e) easily persuaded
166. UNKEMPT: (a) uncombed (b) badly dressed (c) carelessly dressed (d) unwashed (e) untidy
167. BADINAGE: (a) banter (b) abuse (c) mockery (d) obscenity (e) argument
168. LETHARGIC: (a) sluggish (b) idle (c) ill (d) slow (e) dispirited
169. IMPALPABLE: (a) ungraspable (b) impermanent (c) vague (d) dreamlike (e) faultless
170. OBEISANCE: (a) servility (b) obedience (c) deference (d) subordination (e) overlordship
171. BERSERK: (a) mentally upset (b) abnormal (c) abusive (d) unconscious (e) violent and destructive
172. GYRATE: (a) move from place to place (b) dance (c) rotate (d) vacillate (e) move upwards
173. EFFRONTERY: (a) insolence (b) courage (c) shamelessness (d) rudeness (e) lack of respect
174. TESSELLATED: (a) hung around with ribbons (b) decorated with tinsel (c) with horizontal stripes (d) chequered (e) heavily ornamented
175. IMBROGLIO: (a) brawl (b) impasse (c) brothel (d) entanglement (e) crisis
176. EXPEDIENT: (a) device (b) quick (c) that which can be spared (d) imperative (e) appropriate

162. (c)
163. (a)
164. (e)
165. (c)
166. (a)
167. (a)
168. (a)
169. (a)
170. (c)
171. (e)
172. (c)
173. (a)
174. (d)
175. (d)
176. (e)

177. INFRACTION: (a) partitioning (b) violation (c) blood clot (d) conflict (e) fracas

178. CLICHE: (a) terse witty phrase (b) phrase worn out by repetition (c) wise saying (d) appropriate phrase (e) formula

179. FORBEARANCE: (a) sympathy (b) hardheartedness (c) coolness of temper (d) wisdom (e) self-control

180. IDYLLIC: (a) calm and pastoral (b) simple (c) pertaining to nature (d) utopian (e) rustic

181. GRUESOME: (a) murderous (b) bloody (c) horrible (d) excruciating (e) repugnant

182. CRASS: (a) cheap (b) worthless (c) ugly (d) counterfeit (e) unrefined

183. INADVERTENTLY: (a) unintentionally (b) unwisely (c) incautiously (d) inevitably (e) silently

184. FUNEREAL: (a) burial ceremony (b) mournful (c) smoky (d) mystical (e) imaginary

185. PASTICHE: (a) superimposition (b) imitation (c) caricature (d) a small cake (e) a fake

186. BALEFUL: (a) full of hatred (b) menacing (c) nasty (d) sorrowful (e) mysterious

187. ARCHETYPE (pronounced 'arkitype'): (a) representative (b) primitive (c) outdated (d) outmoded (e) prototype

188. HYPERBOLE: (a) praise (b) exaggeration (c) emotional speech (d) empty claim (e) tall talk

189. APPELLATION: (a) plea (b) request (c) appearance (d) title (e) ghost

190. QUEASY: (a) comfortable (b) scrupulous (c) nauseous (d) queer (e) weird

191. CLAIRVOYANT: (a) farsighted (b) amateur (c) having magical powers (d) having mystical experiences (e) having powers of fortune telling

192. UNWONTED: (a) ignored (b) unusual (c) unprecedented (d) undue (e) extraordinary

177. (b)
178. (b)
179. (e)
180. (a)
181. (e)
182. (e)
183. (a)
184. (b)
185. (b)
186. (b)
187. (e)
188. (b)
189. (d)
190. (c)
191. (e)
192. (b)

193. HUSBANDRY: (a) consideration (b) selfishness (c) management (d) control (e) thrift
194. HACKNEYED: (a) stereotyped (b) archaic (c) vulgar (d) appropriate (e) done to death
195. DESCRY: (a) disparage (b) clamour (c) dismiss (d) discover (e) lament
196. FASTIDIOUS: (a) extremely neat (b) hard to please (c) fault-finding (d) watchful of details (e) strict
197. HAPHAZARD: (a) disarranged (b) whimsical (c) slovenly (d) at random (e) untidy
198. DESIDERATUM: (a) important consideration (b) clause (c) conclusion (d) something desired as essential (e) agenda
199. EGOTISM: (a) self-absorption (b) preoccupation with one's own self (c) sense of self-importance (d) self-effacement (e) pride
200. PUTATIVE: (a) provisional (b) alternative (c) assumed (d) prohibited (e) optional
201. SKITTISH: (a) catlike (b) difficult (c) ambiguous (d) playful (e) playing hide and seek
202. MOTLEY: (a) miscellaneous (b) ragged (c) rowdy (d) multicoloured (e) fragile
203. IMPUGN: (a) condemn (b) strike down (c) vilify (d) reject (e) challenge
204. QUANDARY: (a) dilemma (b) grave situation (c) doubt (d) indecisiveness (e) tight spot
205. CEREMONIOUS: (a) marked by impressive ceremony (b) one who has a proper sense of the ceremony (c) pompous (d) formal (e) marked by religious offering
206. CONSTRUE: (a) argue (b) calculate (c) infer (d) interpret (e) complicate
207. FLAGRANT: (a) outrageous (b) devious (c) open (d) obvious (e) criminal
208. HAGGARD: (a) dirty (b) starved (c) ghostlike (d) skin and bones (e) careworn

193. (e)
194. (a)
195. (d)
196. (b)
197. (d)
198. (d)
199. (c)
200. (c)
201. (d)
202. (d)
203. (e)
204. (a)
205. (d)
206. (d)
207. (a)
208. (e)

209. UNWITTING: (a) stupid (b) nonsensical (c) unknowing (d) dull (e) childish
210. CELERITY: (a) clarity of mind (b) speed (c) sharpness of intellect (d) simplicity (e) cleverness
211. RESPITE: (a) rest (b) hatred (c) malignant attitude (d) release (e) acquittal
212. HUMANE: (a) kind (b) concerning humanity (c) human characteristics (d) moist (e) congenial
213. CAUSTIC: (a) sarcastic (b) rude (c) dismissive (d) abusive (e) cautious
214. TENTATIVE: (a) definite (b) hesitant (c) temporary (d) experimental (e) diffident
215. CASTIGATE: (a) flog (b) chastise (c) condemn (d) disprove (e) summarily dismiss
216. HARANGUE: (a) rebuke (b) angry speech (c) exhortation (d) preaching (e) pompous address
217. EFFETE: (a) exhausted (b) empty (c) effeminate (d) corrupted (e) emaciated
218. PATHOLOGICAL: (a) concerning the body (b) concerning the anatomy (c) concerning the mind (d) concerning disease (e) concerning blood, urine, and stool
219. FERVID: (a) feverish (b) heated (c) ferocious (d) honest (e) ardent
220. CATECHISM: (a) political indoctrination (b) religious indoctrination (c) credo (d) question-answer method of instruction (e) liberal approach to moral questions
221. RESIGNED: (a) withdrawn (b) defeated (c) reconciled with (d) submissive (e) fatalistic
222. MORIBUND: (a) unmoving (b) stagnant (c) mortgaged (d) decadent (e) dead
223. ZEALOT: (a) very active person (b) dedicated to a cause (c) fanatic (d) fundamentalist (e) crazed by religious fervour

209. (c)
210. (b)
211. (a)
212. (a)
213. (a)
214. (d)
215. (b)
216. (b)
217. (a)
218. (d)
219. (e)
220. (d)
221. (d)
222. (b)
223. (c)

224. TEMPORIZE: (a) make worldly arrangements (b) impart speed (c) moderate (d) gain time (e) compromise
225. IMPASSIVE: (a) active (b) unmoved (c) untouched (d) inactive (e) dauntless
226. CAROUSAL: (a) indulging in wine, women, and song (b) drunken revelry (c) illicit sex (d) singing the praise of a woman (e) living it up with rum, bum, and concertina
227. FOOLHARDY: (a) stupid (b) unwise (c) rash (d) daredevil (e) inconsiderate
228. SCRUPULOUS: (a) punctilious (b) fault-finding (c) niggling (d) totally honest (e) generous
229. ELUSIVE: (a) difficult to catch (b) imaginary (c) sticky to the touch (d) deceptive (e) unreal
230. QUERULOUS: (a) peevish (b) quarrelsome (c) dissatisfied (d) never satisfied (e) queasy
231. MORDANT: (a) morbid (b) in bad taste (c) flagrant (d) hibernating (e) caustic
232. PARVENU: (a) newly rich (b) parasitical (c) snob (d) the lower classes (e) social climber
233. DENOUEMENT: (a) final outcome (b) dramatic climax (c) anticlimax (d) collapse of the plot (e) progress of a play
234. FAUX PAS (pronounced 'fo pa'): (a) repartee (b) error (c) insult (d) indiscretion (e) unflappability
235. IMPLICATION: (a) involvement (b) inner meaning (c) suggestion (d) clarification (e) entanglement
236. OBFUSCATE: (a) frighten (b) obstruct (c) mislead (d) confuse (e) obscure
237. GROTESQUE: (a) vulgar (b) hilarious (c) fantastically distorted (d) most ugly (e) absurd
238. IMPERVIOUS: (a) impenetrable (b) unaffected (c) native (d) not permanent (e) unmoved

224. (d)
225. (b)
226. (b)
227. (c)
228. (a)
229. (a)
230. (a)
231. (e)
232. (a)
233. (a)
234. (d)
235. (c)
236. (e)
237. (c)
238. (a)

239. SKIMP: (a) shirk work (b) leave out things (c) skip (d) perform shoddily (e) perform carelessly
240. CUISINE: (a) food (b) French cooking (c) style of cooking (d) sophisticated cooking (e) high class food
241. PERMEATE: (a) make permanent (b) cover (c) perpetuate (d) discolour (e) penetrate
242. EMULATE: (a) liquefy (b) apply balm (c) imitate (d) explain (e) emulsify
243. CLAUSTROPHOBIA: (a) fear of confined space (b) fear of unknown persons (c) fear of falling (d) fear of foreigners (e) fear of death by drowning
244. HYPOTHETICAL: (a) possible (b) probable (c) conditional (d) likely (e) unlikely
245. TEMPERATE: (a) low (b) moderate (c) teetotal (d) hot (e) kind
246. MINION: (a) underling (b) boyfriend (c) effeminate companion (d) comrade (e) boon companion
247. JUXTAPOSE: (a) alternate (b) compare (c) place side by side (d) contrast (e) oppose
248. KALEIDOSCOPIC: (a) of a vast range (b) changing shapes and colours (c) revolving (d) panoramic (e) multifarious
249. COMA: (a) a short poem of not more than four lines (b) the shortest punctuation mark (c) one-tenth of a second (d) deep unconsciousness (e) an atom
250. MALADROIT: (a) inexpert (b) ill conceived (c) mistimed (d) clumsy (e) inexperienced
251. PENCHANT: (a) postscript (b) flag (c) passion (d) pungent (e) tendency
252. DISPARAGE: (a) abuse (b) laugh at (c) criticise (d) reject (e) depreciate
253. MAVERICK: (a) rebel (b) a one-day wonder (c) whizzkid (d) genius (e) defector

41

239. (e)
240. (c)
241. (e)
242. (c)
243. (a)
244. (c)
245. (b)
246. (a)
247. (c)
248. (b)
249. (d)
250. (d)
251. (e)
252. (e)
253. (a)

254. STIGMA: (a) slur (b) scandal (c) ill reputation (d) stain (e) mark of disgrace
255. ESCAPADE: (a) scrape (b) daring act of escape (c) a leak (d) protective wall (e) retreat
256. HOLOCAUST: (a) disaster (b) destruction by flood (c) three-dimensional image (d) sweeping away by storm (e) destruction by fire
257. PEREMPTORY: (a) prompt (b) commanding (c) tentative (d) punctual (e) painstaking
258. ADVENTITIOUS: (a) accidental (b) adventurous (c) suspicious (d) happy (e) unusual
259. CALUMNY: (a) slander (b) insult (c) threat (d) criminal offence (e) accusation
260. MALEVOLENT: (a) ill wisher (b) inimical (c) disagreeable (d) miserly (e) wishing evil
261. SENSUAL: (a) bodily (b) sexual (c) pleasing to the senses (d) coarse (e) hedonistic
262. DEPRECATE: (a) disapprove (b) fall in value (c) condemn (d) criticise (e) describe
263. EXTIRPATE: (a) remove completely (b) uproot (c) expunge (d) expiate (e) exorcise
264. SENTENTIOUS: (a) long-winded (b) dismissive (c) authoritative (d) abrupt (e) aphoristic
265. MAELSTROM: (a) squall (b) tornado (c) high wind (d) storm in a teacup (e) whirlpool
266. REPINE: (a) remember (b) repent (c) rest (d) long for (e) fret
267. ODIOUS: (a) smelly (b) ugly (c) horrible (d) sad (e) offensive
268. SYLVAN: (a) Utopian (b) silvery (c) innocent (d) pastoral (e) wooded
269. CANARD: (a) slander (b) false report (c) practical joke (d) defamation (e) faux pas
270. SINISTER: (a) hateful (b) evil (c) harmful (d) treacherous (e) nasty
271. BIZARRE: (a) frightening (b) supernatural (c) violent (d) odd (e) mysterious

254. (e)
255. (a)
256. (e)
257. (b)
258. (a)
259. (a)
260. (e)
261. (a)
262. (a)
263. (a)
264. (e)
265. (e)
266. (e)
267. (e)
268. (e)
269. (b)
270. (b)
271. (d)

272. FREEBOOTER: (a) parasite (b) collector of free handouts (c) one who lives off plunder (d) freedom fighter in South Africa (e) one who rides roughshod over others

273. GUMPTION: (a) commonsense (b) patience (c) impudence (d) presence of mind (e) power

274. AGNOSTIC: (a) mystic (b) unbeliever (c) non-christian (d) sceptical of the existence of God (e) one who neither believes nor disbelieves in the existence of God

275. MISCONSTRUE: (a) misinterpret (b) misspell (c) misconstruct sentences (d) misdirect (e) mismatch

276. CENTURION: (a) one who is at least one hundred years old (b) a cricketer who has scored a century (c) one who has made 100 grand (100,000 dollars or pounds) (d) a Roman commander of 100 soldiers (e) a Mafia godfather who has eliminated at least a hundred of his enemies

277. KLEPTOMANIAC: (a) compulsive thief (b) compulsive lecher (c) compulsive drinker (d) compulsive liar (e) compulsive gambler

278. MEANDER: (a) climb (b) undulate (c) stray (d) wander aimlessly (e) cut across

279. IDIOSYNCRASY: (a) quirk (b) idiocy (c) perversity (d) proneness (e) wrongheadedness

280. FRACTIOUS: (a) divisible (b) broken (c) invalid (d) temperamental (e) unruly

281. AGGRANDIZE: (a) make enemies (b) increase (c) terrify (d) grind to a powder (e) punish

282. NIGGARDLY: (a) cowardly (b) stingy (c) mean (d) ungrateful (e) ungentlemanly

283. CATHARTIC: (a) decongestant (b) blood purifying (c) cough loosening (d) anti-allergic (e) purgative

272. (c)
273. (a)
274. (d)
275. (a)
276. (d)
277. (a)
278. (d)
279. (a)
280. (e)
281. (b)
282. (b)
283. (e)

284. LACHRYMOSE: (a) pathetic (b) well-oiled (c) thought-provoking (d) tearful (e) complaining
285. SWARTHY: (a) fat (b) sturdy (c) dirty (d) dark (e) reddish
286. ABSOLVE: (a) dilute (b) find a solution (c) reduce (d) pardon (e) rectify
287. LANGUOR: (a) despondency (b) weariness (c) laziness (d) feverishness (e) hypnosis
288. INVIDIOUS: (a) indivisible (b) unfavourable (c) discriminating (d) unfair (e) superficial
289. OFFICIOUS: (a) bureaucratic (b) helpful (c) obstructive (d) meddlesome (e) servile
290. PHILANDER: (a) womanize (b) squander (c) plunder (d) flirt (e) physically intimidate
291. NOXIOUS: (a) foul (b) objectionable (c) nasty (d) poisonous (e) suffocating
292. IMMACULATE: (a) white (b) spotless (c) perfect (d) completely honest (e) pregnant outside wedlock
293. NUBILE: (a) lissom (b) prone (c) handsome (d) dark (e) marriageable
294. NURTURE: (a) culture (b) breed (c) feed (d) experiment (e) develop
295. DOTAGE: (a) ill health (b) senility (c) old age (d) distant past (e) mythical past
296. OAF: (a) giant (b) lout (c) country bumpkin (d) goon (e) uneducated fellow
297. OBDURATE: (a) perverse (b) disobedient (c) hostile (d) arrogant (e) stubborn
298. ALIMONY: (a) once-for-all settlement (b) kickback (c) divorce payment (d) interest (e) blackmail
299. MALINGER: (a) delay (b) shirk (c) accuse (d) abuse (e) waste time
300. CAVIL: (a) protest (b) rebel (c) raise petty objections (d) criticise unnecessarily (e) vilify

284. (d)
285. (d)
286. (d)
287. (b)
288. (c)
289. (d)
290. (d)
291. (d)
292. (b)
293. (e)
294. (c)
295. (b)
296. (b)
297. (e)
298. (c)
299. (b)
300. (c)

301. HEDONIST: (a) one who lives well (b) one who does not believe in God (c) one who is not a Christian (d) one who does not believe in afterlife (e) one who believes that pleasure is the chief good
302. CHARLATAN: (a) quack (b) rascal (c) deceiver (d) ignorant (e) low-born
303. LARCENY: (a) robbery (b) theft (c) murder (d) rape (e) kidnap
304. ACCRETION: (a) improvement (b) increase (c) decay (d) attachment (e) speeding up
305. DISQUISITION: (a) thesis (b) discourse (c) lecture (d) debate (e) religious address
306. STRIATED: (a) uneven (b) undulating (c) particoloured (d) streaked with paint (e) striped
307. LUGUBRIOUS: (a) clumsy (b) disoriented (c) complicated (d) doleful (e) messy
308. ICONOCLAST: (a) social reformer (b) religious reformer (c) destroyer of superstitious beliefs (d) destroyer of sacred objects (e) a stormy character
309. ARROGATE: (a) rectify (b) assign (c) claim unjustly (d) surrender (e) ask questions
310. NONCHALANCE: (a) unashamed behaviour (b) smartness (c) lack of fear (d) bravado (e) indifference
311. WIZENED: (a) very old (b) sagacious (c) bold (d) embittered (e) shrivelled
312. PANEGYRIC: (a) eulogy (b) certificate (c) decoration (d) medicine (e) restorative
313. LURID: (a) obscene (b) sensational (c) bloody (d) savage (e) vivid
314. INIQUITOUS: (a) unequal (b) conflicting (c) wicked (d) improper (e) discordant
315. STATIC: (a) stable (b) inactive (c) energetic (d) stationary (e) restful
316. MACABRE: (a) murderous (b) ghastly (c) violent (d) sick (e) deadly

301. (e)
302. (a)
303. (b)
304. (b)
305. (b)
306. (e)
307. (d)
308. (d)
309. (c)
310. (e)
311. (e)
312. (a)
313. (b)
314. (c)
315. (d)
316. (b)

317. TAWDRY: (a) vulgar (b) cheap (c) seemingly witty (d) expensive but in bad taste (e) showy but worthless
318. ASTRINGENT: (a) harsh (b) abusive (c) logical (d) obscure (e) bitter
319. TEMERITY: (a) nervousness (b) fear (c) rashness (d) boldness (e) arrogance
320. IRASCIBLE: (a) harsh (b) unpredictable (c) quick (d) irritable (e) unbending
321. STENTORIAN: (a) authoritative (b) ear-piercing (c) extremely powerful (d) harsh (e) stony
322. BRAVADO: (a) bravery (b) courage (c) might (d) false courage (e) swagger
323. OBLIQUE: (a) indirect (b) opposite (c) difficult (d) sophisticated (e) obscure
324. MACHINATION: (a) contrivance (b) structure (c) intrigue (d) management (e) tooling
325. PANDER: (a) libertine (b) pimp (c) hawker (d) whore (e) squander away
326. WRY: (a) distorted (b) desiccated (c) pained (d) amused (e) sarcastic
327. DISSIMULATE: (a) to lead a loose life (b) drink excessively (c) disintegrate (d) disperse (e) dissemble
328. ITINERANT: (a) repetitious (b) irrelevant (c) tour programme (d) irritating (e) travelling
329. ONEROUS: (a) unpleasant (b) difficult (c) oppressive (d) time-consuming (e) irritating
330. XENOPHOBIA: (a) morbid dislike of women (b) morbid dislike of bearded men (c) morbid dislike of the old (d) morbid dislike of foreigners (e) morbid dislike of war
331. NONPLUSSED: (a) confounded (b) disqualified (c) puzzled (d) disconnected (e) dissatisfied
332. HERESY: (a) anti-establishment opinion (b) untruth (c) evil belief (d) abusing the Papacy (e) holding opinions contrary to popular belief

317. (e)
318. (a)
319. (c)
320. (d)
321. (c)
322. (e)
323. (a)
324. (c)
325. (b)
326. (a)
327. (e)
328. (e)
329. (c)
330. (d)
331. (a)
332. (a)

333. STRINGENT: (a) severe (b) strict (c) constricting (d) violent (e) savage
334. JADED: (a) surfeited (b) lacklustre (c) faded (d) exhausted (e) ornamented
335. DENIGRATE: (a) denounce (b) ridicule (c) dismiss (d) vilify (e) blacken
336. STOIC: (a) impassive (b) brave (c) perseverant (d) able to endure great hardship (e) virtuous
337. QUIZZICAL: (a) quizzes about Calcutta (b) of quizzes (c) perplexing (d) mocking (e) puzzled
338. ECLECTICISM: (a) choosing to be among the elite (b) rejection of the idea that an elite should exist (c) an attitude which changes radically from time to time (d) forming an attitude composed of elements drawn from various sources (e) an attitude which considers that the best can never be achieved
339. MAWKISH: (a) sardonical (b) falsely sentimental (c) hypocritical (d) superficial (e) immature
340. DEFALCATE: (a) fail to repay a loan (b) delay payment (c) fail to keep promise (d) keep false account books (e) embezzle
341. IMPUDENT: (a) arrogant (b) improvident (c) impious (d) impertinent (e) unwise
342. PORTENTOUS: (a) pompous (b) officious (c) official (d) ominous (e) disastrous
343. GREGARIOUS: (a) grazing (b) solitary (c) inconstant (d) sociable (e) collective
344. CARPING: (a) complaining (b) abusing (c) fault-finding (d) harshly criticising (e) being petty minded
345. SOPHISTRY: (a) sophistication (b) philosophical reasoning (c) false reasoning (d) mystification (e) legalistic reasoning
346. DEFECATE: (a) efface (b) make ugly, walls etc., by writing on them (c) damage public monuments (d) distort (e) shit

333. (b)
334. (a)
335. (e)
336. (a)
337. (d)
338. (d)
339. (b)
340. (e)
341. (d)
342. (d)
343. (d)
344. (c)
345. (c)
346. (e)

347. TATTY: (a) torn (b) vulgar (c) shabby
(d) cheap (e) mean
348. BAROQUE: (a) primitive (b) Turkish (c) vulgar (d) highly ornamented (e) showy
349. REPROACH: (a) proposition (b) rebuke
(c) remind (d) condemn (e) criticise
350. IMMUTABLE: (a) that which can be changed
(b) temporary (c) mortal (d) eternal (e) unchangeable
351. FRAUGHT: (a) frightened (b) fried (c) tied up
(d) overflowing (e) filled
352. PETULANT: (a) moody (b) angry (c) sentimental (d) annoyed (e) irritable
353. DEPLOY: (a) use with a special purpose
(b) make good use of (c) fight with the enemy
(d) deceive the enemy (e) arrange troops
strategically
354. COLLATE: (a) gather together (b) compare
critically (c) relate one thing to another (d) pass
through a sieve (e) evaluate
355. ILLUSORY: (a) bright (b) deceptive (c) misleading (d) picturesque (e) dreamlike
356. CHATTEL: (a) wife and children (b) domestic
animals (c) ancestral property (d) property tax
(e) personal property
357. ESOTERIC: (a) supernatural (b) primitive
(c) abstruse (d) mystical (e) pertaining to magic
358. TERSE: (a) rude (b) concise (c) dismissive
(d) curt (e) acid
359. INSOUCIANT: (a) smooth (b) faultless
(c) smart (d) unconcerned (e) disrespectful
360. CRUX: (a) apex (b) insoluble problem (c) the
heart of a problem (d) a point of no return
(e) general nature
361. UMBRAGE: (a) punishment (b) oversensitivity
(c) sense of being ignored (d) sense of being
unjustly treated (e) sense of injury

347. (c)
348. (d)
349. (b)
350. (e)
351. (e)
352. (e)
353. (e)
354. (b)
355. (b)
356. (e)
357. (c)
358. (b)
359. (d)
360. (c)
361. (e)

362. IMPORTUNATE: (a) begging (b) unlucky (c) rash (d) inconsiderate (e) insisting
363. FULMINATE: (a) fume (b) abuse (c) rant (d) explode (e) fulfil
364. INCARNATE: (a) undying (b) born again (c) imprisoned (d) of red colour (e) personified
365. ENGENDER: (a) to father (b) to put in peril (c) to preach (d) to promote (e) to support
366. UBIQUITOUS: (a) elusive (b) being everywhere (c) ambiguous (d) using both hands equally well (e) that which can serve many purposes
367. BURLY: (a) fat (b) thickset (c) athletic (d) strong (e) with a thick moustache
368. FLAMBOYANT: (a) flourishing (b) florid (c) flying (d) extravagant (e) notorious
369. THERAPEUTIC: (a) cleansing (b) curative (c) medicinal (d) health-giving (e) ameliorative
370. EFFULGENT: (a) overflowing (b) radiant (c) in full bloom (d) bountiful (e) rich with divine grace
371. SCURRILOUS: (a) spiteful (b) obscenely abusive (c) vehement (d) defamatory (e) abusive and violent
372. FRIVOLITY: (a) humour (b) frolic (c) lack of good sense (d) lack of seriousness (e) lack of good manners
373. SOPORIFIC: (a) congenial (b) harmful (c) lethargic (d) sleepy (e) blissful
374. COY: (a) sensitive (b) coquettish (c) flirtatious (d) deceiving (e) sophisticated
375. IMPRIMATUR: (a) permission to extend stay (b) permission to trade (c) permission to join priestly brotherhood (d) permission to print (e) honourable discharge
376. LIAISON: (a) friendship (b) give and take (c) negotiation (d) adultery (e) conspiracy

362. (e)
363. (d)
364. (e)
365. (a)
366. (b)
367. (b)
368. (b)
369. (b)
370. (b)
371. (b)
372. (d)
373. (d)
374. (b)
375. (d)
376. (d)

377. GRANDIOSE: (a) pompous (b) bombastic (c) showy (d) grand (e) imposing
378. BOURGEOIS: (a) traders (b) reactionary (c) petty minded (d) middle-class (e) evil servants
379. EXECRATE: (a) denounce (b) defecate (c) curse (d) abominate (e) extort
380. INTERDICT: (a) condemn (b) connect (c) exchange (d) proclaim (e) prohibit
381. DIALECTIC: (a) political belief (b) philosophy (c) controversy (d) argument (e) debate
382. SOLECISM: (a) consolation (b) eagerness (c) solemnity (d) using pedantic words (e) grammatical error
383. COLLUDE: (a) conclude (b) co-operate (c) decide (d) conspire (e) persuade
384. PRIM: (a) demure (b) proper (c) prudent (d) neat (e) exact
385. LIBIDO: (a) licentiousness (b) lust (c) psychology (d) obscenity (e) sexual urge
386. DEIGN: (a) show mercy (b) deny (c) attempt (d) try (e) condescend
387. SATED: (a) jaded (b) pampered (c) cloyed (d) tired (e) bored
388. EXECRABLE: (a) that which can be abstracted (b) hot-headed (c) deserving punishment (d) very bad (e) dishonest
389. FATUOUS: (a) obese (b) sycophantic (c) foolish (d) self-satisfied (e) meaningless
390. INCOMPATIBLE: (a) inharmonious (b) unhealthy (c) unfriendly (d) unfavourable (e) incorrigible
391. PLAINTIVE: (a) mournful (b) complaining (c) simple (d) telling a sad story (e) reminiscing
392. EQUIVOCAL: (a) one similar to another (b) lying (c) doubtful (d) that which lends itself to several interpretations (e) ambiguous

377. (e)
378. (d)
379. (c)
380. (e)
381. (e)
382. (e)
383. (d)
384. (a)
385. (e)
386. (e)
387. (c)
388. (d)
389. (c)
390. (a)
391. (a)
392. (c)

393. CUL DE SAC: (a) love nest (b) attic (c) blind alley (d) secluded place (e) hovel
394. RETRIBUTION: (a) chastisement (b) compensation (c) confirmation (d) return (e) revenge
395. EXEGESIS: (a) discourse (b) thesis (c) critical explanation (d) exhortation (e) correction of text
396. SOJOURN: (a) go on a journey (b) go to a foreign country (c) departing (d) temporary stay (e) travelling from place to place
397. TRIVIA: (a) nonsense (b) trinkets (c) cheap things (d) unimportant matter (e) trifles
398. INVETERATE: (a) incorrigible (b) inevitable (c) unvarying (d) incontrovertible (e) hardened
399. SINECURE: (a) pensionary payment (b) golden handshake (c) a permanent post with total job security (d) some job found for a nephew (e) paid post with minimal duties
400. CULPABLE: (a) blameworthy (b) accidental (c) responsible (d) deliberate (e) forgivable
401. TATTLE: (a) carry tales (b) divulge secrets (c) cackle (d) gossip (e) raise a hue and cry
402. EXPATIATE: (a) explain away (b) show compassion (c) leave one's native country (d) do penance (e) elaborate on
403. SLATTERN: (a) a whore (b) a woman with easy morals (c) a slut (d) a lazy woman (e) a foul-mouthed woman
404. TARDY: (a) stingy (b) slow (c) unwilling (d) mean (e) difficult
405. CUPIDITY: (a) lust (b) love (c) attractiveness (d) greed (e) curiosity
406. INEPT: (a) inappropriate (b) clumsy (c) stupid (d) difficult (e) indecent
407. GERIATRIC: (a) world traveller (b) strengthening (c) elderly (d) senile (e) foot soldier

393. (c)
394. (e)
395. (c)
396. (d)
397. (e)
398. (e)
399. (e)
400. (a)
401. (d)
402. (e)
403. (c)
404. (b)
405. (d)
406. (b)
407. (c)

408. PIQUANT: (a) embarrassing (b) critical (c) tense (d) agreeably pungent (e) sarcastic
409. INCONTINENT: (a) unrepentant (b) unrestrained (c) unmerciful (d) weakwilled (e) dissatisfied
410. FATALISM: (a) rate of mortality (b) extremism (c) grievousness (d) belief in predeterminism (e) surrender to misfortune
411. SERENDIPITY: (a) stealth (b) making fortunate dicoveries by accident (c) knack of recovering lost articles (d) clairvoyance (e) serenity
412. FERVOUR: (a) zeal (b) feverish activity (c) truthfulness (d) feverishness (e) excitement
413. OVERT: (a) simple (b) complicated (c) open (d) declared (e) terminated
414. ANALGESIC: (a) headache pill (b) forgetful (c) causing loss of consciousness (d) stimulant (e) causing inability to feel pain
415. RISIBLE: (a) ludicrous (b) excitable (c) loud (d) tending to raise (e) hot-tempered
416. DAPPLED: (a) sparkling (b) spotted (c) multicoloured (d) rippling (e) paint crudely applied
417. INSULAR: (a) protected (b) isolated (c) secular (d) diplomatic (e) hygienic
418. CONNOISSEUR: (a) art expert (b) art critic (c) expert on antiques (d) judge of good food (e) knowledgeable about the fine arts
419. POIGNANT: (a) touching (b) sharp (c) pathetic (d) unbearable (e) maximal
420. CONTROVERT: (a) contradict (b) refer back (c) sabotage (d) accept (e) violate
421. SHAMBLES: (a) ruins (b) devastation (c) slaughterhouse (d) electrocution chamber (e) torture chamber
422. EXOTIC: (a) mysterious (b) confined to a select few (c) concerned with magic (d) of rare excellence (e) foreign

408. (d)
409. (b)
410. (d)
411. (b)
412. (a)
413. (c)
414. (e)
415. (a)
416. (b)
417. (b)
418. (a)
419. (b)
420. (a)
421. (c)
422. (e)

423. PHLEGMATIC: (a) calm (b) calculated (c) crafty (d) dilatory (e) easy victim of coughs and colds
424. OSTENSIBLE: (a) reasonable (b) just (c) tenable (d) showy (e) apparent
425. EXTOL: (a) exalt (b) elaborate (c) critically examine (d) toll-free (e) extend
426. SQUALID: (a) repulsive (b) malodorous (c) flyblown (d) filthy (e) disreputable
427. CATALYST: (a) that which causes a change without changing itself (b) that which breaks up things (c) a cause that binds together conflicting ideologies (d) opportunist who is prepared to flatter his ideological enemies (e) one who challenges established notions
428. PICARESQUE: (a) rambling (b) a novel with epic dimensions (c) a novel with changes of locale (d) an indecent fiction (e) a novel depicting adventures of rogues
429. BONANZA: (a) public burning of books (b) reduction sale (c) unexpected luck (d) massive sale (e) festive season
430. DEADPAN: (a) frightening (b) ugly (c) morose (d) expressionless (e) cadaverous
431. SOLICITOUS: (a) making appeals (b) giving solace (c) canvassing (d) anxious (e) friendly
432. COGENT: (a) reasonable (b) lucid (c) acceptable (d) logical (e) convincing
433. GLOWER: (a) shine brightly (b) seethe with anger (c) fume (d) scowl (e) gather together
434. AMORPHOUS: (a) vague (b) shapeless (c) fragrant (d) stifling (e) confused
435. DEFILE: (a) damage (b) violate (c) destroy (d) blaspheme (e) ravish
436. TITILLATE: (a) rouse (b) scratch (c) smart (d) tickle (e) incite prurience

423. (a)
424. (e)
425. (a)
426. (d)
427. (a)
428. (e)
429. (c)
430. (d)
431. (d)
432. (e)
433. (d)
434. (b)
435. (b)
436. (d)

437. GOURMAND: (a) epicure (b) connoisseur of food (c) potbellied (d) one who gobbles food (e) go-getter
438. TRANSMUTE: (a) make silent (b) transfer (c) change (d) remit (e) elevate
439. COLOPHON: (a) title page of a book (b) primitive listening device (c) printer's or publisher's device (d) the royal seal (e) ornamental device at the end of a book
440. PRECIPITATE: (a) hesitant (b) quick (c) rash (d) impulsive (e) disastrous
441. CHAMELEON: (a) a changeable person (b) an effeminate boy (c) one who is dressed up like a tart (d) one who is afflicted with leprosy (e) a mellifluous singer
442. RECIDIVISM: (a) relapse into infantility (b) revisionism (c) relapse into crime (d) loss of faith in God (e) recantation
443. SNIGGER: (a) sly laugh (b) sarcastic laugh (c) derisive laugh (d) noisy laugh (e) secret laugh
444. COHORT: (a) gangster's mate (b) group of soldiers (c) assistant (d) group leader (e) mistress
445. PLATITUDE: (a) unsolicited advice (b) words of wisdom (c) commonplaces (d) hypothesis (e) self-evident truth
446. TOADY: (a) muscleman (b) timeserver (c) slave (d) obsequious hanger-on (e) insignificant fellow
447. RECONDITE: (a) abstruse (b) familiar (c) repetitious (d) reconciled (e) difficult
448. FETISH: (a) an evil object (b) embodiment of the devil (c) a talisman (d) embodiment of magical power (e) superstition
449. PREDILECTION: (a) tendency (b) dilemma (c) direction (d) predisposition (e) preference

437. (a)
438. (c)
439. (c)
440. (c)
441. (a)
442. (c)
443. (a)
444. (b)
445. (c)
446. (d)
447. (a)
448. (d)
449. (e)

450. COIFFURE: (a) hair gathered in a bun (b) stylish clothes (c) hair styling (d) quality food (e) French salad
451. PRESUMPTUOUS: (a) ambitious (b) ostentatious (c) cocksure (d) forward (e) disrespectful
452. EQUIVOCATE: (a) lie (b) make contradictory statements (c) deny (d) make meaningless statements (e) vacillate
453. GARISH: (a) colourful (b) crude (c) gaudy (d) of the colour of green (e) loud
454. SANCTIMONIOUS: (a) saintly (b) pious (c) immoral (d) approved (e) hypocritically devout
455. INNUENDO: (a) insinuation (b) metaphor (c) accusation (d) slander (e) aspersion
456. DISTRAIT: (a) agitated with mental conflict (b) sick with fear (c) absent-minded (d) hopeless (e) overcome with grief
457. EXALT: (a) celebrate (b) praise (c) raise high (d) deify (e) feel happy
458. CONTRITE: (a) perverse (b) repentant (c) opposed (d) agreeable (e) commonplace
459. SANGUINE: (a) absolutely certain (b) cheerful (c) bloody (d) sacred (e) sardonic
460. PREMONITION: (a) forewarning (b) foreknowledge (c) fear (d) doubt (e) mystical knowledge
461. ERRATIC: (a) sexually stimulating (b) wandering (c) mistaken (d) unpredictable (e) well-read
462. LISTLESS: (a) inattentive (b) incautious (c) anonymous (d) unresponsive (e) languid
463. GINGIVITIS: (a) infection of the pancreas (b) inflammation of the thyroid gland (c) inflammation of the joints (d) inflammation of the gums (e) an infection of the bladder

450. (c)
451. (d)
452. (a)
453. (c)
454. (e)
455. (a)
456. (c)
457. (c)
458. (b)
459. (b)
460. (a)
461. (d)
462. (e)
463. (d)

464. PLAUSIBLE: (a) possible (b) probable (c) truthful (d) supported by facts (e) seemingly reasonable

465. EPITOME (pronounced 'epitomi'): (a) a lengthy work (b) the most important work of a writer (c) standard of excellence (d) combination of virtues (e) embodiment

466. TANTRUM: (a) rowdy behaviour (b) uncontrollable behaviour (c) outburst of bad temper (d) spoilt behaviour (e) rage

467. DECADENCE: (a) a state of complete degeneration of moral values (b) death (c) worsening (d) decay (e) corruption

468. ENTOMOLOGY: (a) study of plants (b) study of crop production (c) study of soil fertility (d) study of insects (e) study of crop diseases

469. MUNDANE: (a) commonplace (b) inferior (c) cheap (d) worldly (e) bodily

470. EXTRANEOUS: (a) abnormal (b) foreign (c) extra (d) extraordinary (e) inessential

471. PHILISTINE: (a) petit bourgeois (b) barbarous (c) belonging to another religion (d) uncultured (e) vulgar

472. ABJURE: (a) deny (b) postpone (c) condemn (d) cancel (e) renounce

473. SHACKLES: (a) bonds (b) subjugation (c) constraint (d) chain (e) strong leather bonds

474. GIMCRACK: (a) rabble rousing (b) corrupt (c) cheap (d) gimmicky (e) smart

475. DEBONAIR: (a) gay (b) smart (c) charming (d) handsome (e) winning

476. SIMIAN: (a) lion-like (b) august (c) regal (d) saintly (e) monkey-like

477. GERMANE: (a) Germanic (b) capable of sprouting (c) irrelevant (d) hostile (e) pertinent

478. MUNIFICENT: (a) extremely efficient (b) well-armed (c) grand (d) magnanimous (e) bountiful

464. (e)
465. (e)
466. (c)
467. (d)
468. (d)
469. (d)
470. (e)
471. (d)
472. (e)
473. (d)
474. (c)
475. (c)
476. (e)
477. (e)
478. (e)

479. FICKLE: (a) weak (b) quick (c) unfaithful (d) false (e) inconstant
480. OBSOLETE: (a) archaic (b) outlandish (c) modish (d) decaying (e) outmoded
481. ARTEFACT: (a) objects of daily use (b) works of art (c) forms of artistic activity (d) inferior art objects (e) products of primitive culture
482. DECIPHER: (a) understand (b) decode (c) read (d) take a decision (e) develop
483. TRANSGRESS: (a) infringe (b) break promise (c) commit adultery (d) bear false witness (e) occupy forcibly
484. INSIDIOUS: (a) tortuous (b) insipid (c) tricky (d) complicated (e) treacherous
485. DEBUTANTE: (a) a female model (b) a society woman who is the star of a show (c) a young woman making an entrance into society (d) an unmarried woman above thirty who is the mistress of her house (e) a titled bride
486. REFRACTORY: (a) fractional (b) contrary (c) contradictory (d) unmanageable (e) breakaway
487. GESTICULATE: (a) chew (b) digest (c) gesture (d) lecture (e) keep alive
488. FIGMENT: (a) colour (b) imagination (c) fiction (d) fabrication (e) creation
489. ASSAY: (a) a short discourse (b) attempt (c) explain (d) evaluate (e) contradict
490. PREVARICATE: (a) lie (b) present specious argument (c) verify (d) vouch for (e) anticipate
491. DIDACTIC: (a) dedicated to a noble cause (b) an act with a purpose (c) devoted (d) worshipful (e) aiming to teach
492. DECREPIT: (a) worn out (b) outmoded (c) inactive (d) insane (e) unable to move
493. SARDONIC: (a) scornful (b) humorous (c) disbelieving (d) mournful (e) slow

479. (e)
480. (e)
481. (e)
482. (b)
483. (a)
484. (e)
485. (c)
486. (d)
487. (c)
488. (d)
489. (d)
490. (a)
491. (e)
492. (a)
493. (a)

494. FACADE: (a) appearance (b) front (c) easy accomplishment (d) pretence (e) complication
495. SMIRK: (a) self-satisfied smile (b) silly smile (c) mocking smile (d) superior smile (e) knowledgeable smile
496. EXUBERANCE: (a) luxuriance (b) rowdiness (c) excessive cordiality (d) optimism (e) exhibitionism
497. MISOGYNIST: (a) cynic (b) hater of mankind (c) strict puritan (d) pessimist (e) hater of women
498. PARAMETER: (a) circumference (b) limit (c) definition (d) blank verse (e) parabola
499. BANAL: (a) malicious (b) stupid (c) commonplace (d) indecent (e) harmful
500. UNFEIGNED: (a) unamused (b) infallible (c) real (d) genuine (e) unaffected
501. CARCINOGEN: (a) cigarette smoke (b) diesel fumes (c) harmful chemicals (d) nuclear radiation (e) cancer producing agent
502. SLUGGARD: (a) slow (b) lazy (c) idle (d) backward (e) untidy
503. BANTER: (a) tease (b) criticise (c) rebuke (d) exchange insults (e) mock
504. GIBE: (a) chatter (b) jeer (c) make faces (d) scold (e) gesture
505. TURBID: (a) swollen (b) muddy (c) feverish (d) highly emotive (e) grandiose
506. CONTENTIOUS: (a) satisfied (b) angry (c) quarrelsome (d) suspicious (e) assertive
507. SYCOPHANT: (a) toady (b) worshipper (c) admirer (d) fan (e) servile person
508. ATAVISTIC: (a) showing signs of return to a primitive type (b) self-absorbed (c) withdrawn from everyday life (d) superstitious (e) totally insensitive
509. OBTRUDE: (a) obstruct (b) intrude (c) push forward (d) break into (e) raise objection

494. (b)
495. (b)
496. (a)
497. (e)
498. (b)
499. (c)
500. (d)
501. (e)
502. (b)
503. (a)
504. (b)
505. (b)
506. (c)
507. (a)
508. (a)
509. (c)

510. **CAJOLE:** (a) demand (b) flatter (c) threaten (d) coax (e) urge
511. **SERRATED:** (a) saw-edged (b) broken up (c) sharp-edged (d) uneven (e) undulating
512. **COLLOQUY:** (a) conversation (b) negotiation (c) silent dialogue in one's mind (d) dialogue with God (e) soliloquy
513. **EXORCISE:** (a) expel (b) cure (c) complicate (d) examine critically (e) urge
514. **POLEMICAL:** (a) satirical (b) controversial (c) objectionable (d) blasphemous (e) theological
515. **RUMINATE:** (a) reminisce (b) ponder (c) regret (d) repine (e) consider
516. **CONTINENCE:** (a) repentance (b) continuity (c) sorrow (d) restraint (e) chastity
517. **STALWART:** (a) tall (b) sturdy (c) leading (d) diehard (e) distinguished
518. **GAUCHE:** (a) gaudy (b) garish (c) highly colourful (d) tactless (e) naive
519. **PARANOIA:** (a) inferiority complex (b) superiority complex (c) persecution mania (d) paralysis (e) parapsychological experience
520. **CARNAL:** (a) of the flesh (b) sinful (c) adulterous (d) forbidden pleasures (e) sexual
521. **SUBSTANTIVE:** (a) major (b) solid (c) steady (d) permanent (e) considerable
522. **CONTEND:** (a) argue (b) swear (c) reply (d) plead (e) assert
523. **UNGAINLY:** (a) ugly (b) unprofitable (c) awkward (d) unbalanced (e) unseemly
524. **PROBITY:** (a) truth (b) good sense (c) uprightness (d) holiness (e) modesty
525. **OCCULT:** (a) secret (b) closed (c) pagan (d) religious (e) diabolical
526. **FLORID:** (a) flushed (b) vulgar (c) loud (d) crude (e) unsophisticated

510. (d)
511. (a)
512. (a)
513. (a)
514. (b)
515. (b)
516. (e)
517. (b)
518. (d)
519. (c)
520. (a)
521. (d)
522. (e)
523. (c)
524. (c)
525. (a)
526. (a)

527. RUE: (a) ponder (b) be nostalgic (c) regret
(d) ruminate (e) repent
528. CLOISTER: (a) small room (b) confined space
(c) monastery (d) room of worship (e) study
room
529. SALUTARY: (a) respectful (b) favourable
(c) wholesome (d) strong (e) proper
530. OBSTREPEROUS: (a) obstructive (b) rough
(c) obstinate (d) divisive (e) insolent
531. ANOMIE: (a) lack of social or moral standards
(b) petrification (c) a state of deliberate suspension of movement (d) lawlessness (e) lack of
animation
532. FULSOME: (a) comprehensive (b) disgustingly
insincere (c) fragrant (d) flattering
(e) malodorous
533. RHETORICAL: (a) metaphorical (b) poetical
(c) exaggerated (d) bombastic (e) empty
534. EUTHANASIA: (a) birth control (b) creation
of a healthy race through selective breeding
(c) artificial insemination (d) mercy killing
(e) genetic engineering
535. CHEQUERED: (a) distinguished (b) marked by
progressive success (c) marked by fluctuations
of fortune (d) highly interesting (e) marked by
sensational experiences
536. GAMBIT: (a) game of chess (b) jump about
(c) a bait to catch or shoot wild animals
(d) opening move (e) a gambling den
537. ROCOCO: (a) artificial (b) effeminate (c) decadent (d) Italianate (e) ornate
538. CORUSCATING: (a) eating away (b) rippling
(c) acid (d) glittering (e) fluctuating
539. PERSONABLE: (a) presentable (b) smart
(c) attractive (d) with a strong personality
(e) clever
540. ADEPT: (a) disciple (b) practitioner (c) ac-
curate (d) apprentice (e) skilled

527. (c)
528. (c)
529. (c)
530. (b)
531. (a)
532. (b)
533. (d)
534. (d)
535. (c)
536. (d)
537. (e)
538. (d)
539. (c)
540. (e)

541. TRANSVESTITE: (a) one who behaves in the manner of the opposite sex (b) homosexual (c) one who desires to become a member of the opposite sex (d) a eunuch (e) one who derives sexual pleasure from wearing the clothes of the opposite sex

542. COLLAGE: (a) institution of technical education (b) flower arrangement (c) collection of small objects of art (d) water colour painting (e) artwork of fragments of diverse material

543. SUPERCILIOUS: (a) sycophantic (b) intimidating (c) superior (d) disrespectful (e) contemptuous

544. COERCE: (a) beat up (b) force (c) unite (d) persuade (e) invade

545. TURPITUDE: (a) laziness (b) lack of principle (c) perversity (d) depravity (e) slowness

546. SMATTERING: (a) superficial knowledge (b) sprinkling (c) destruction (d) adornment (e) mixing up

547. ATTRITION: (a) revenge (b) extermination (c) mercy (d) wearing down (e) savagery

548. FURTIVE: (a) secretive (b) noiseless (c) criminal (d) furry (e) cautious

549. RESUSCITATE: (a) expel (b) repair (c) renew (d) reconsider (e) revive

550. FUSSY: (a) noisy (b) troublemaking (c) very particular about detail (d) seldom satisfied (e) fault-finding

551. FLACCID: (a) fat (b) cold (c) flat (d) flabby (e) rancid

552. PROSELYTIZE: (a) break down into constituent elements (b) help congeal (c) precipitate (d) convert (e) analyse

553. AWRY (pronounced 'aw-rai'): (a) strange (b) ghostly (c) askew (d) unnatural (e) disarranged

541. (e)
542. (e)
543. (e)
544. (b)
545. (d)
546. (a)
547. (d)
548. (a)
549. (e)
550. (c)
551. (d)
552. (d)
553. (c)

554. PSYCHOPATHIC: (a) subconscious (b) sensitive (c) clairvoyant (d) delirious (e) mentally deranged

555. GAMESTER: (a) gambler (b) one of the very best players of a game (c) a laying hen (d) hoodlum (e) gangster

556. OPPROBRIOUS: (a) disgraceful (b) deserving censure (c) servile (d) hateful (e) unpleasant

557. CYNOSURE: (a) object of popular hatred (b) important person (c) object of attention (d) dust particle in the eye (e) pleasing to the eyes

558. SPECIOUS: (a) roomy (b) special (c) of a kind (d) palpably false (e) seemingly plausible

559. CACHE: (a) place of hiding (b) a collection of something illegal (c) recovered game (d) resting place (e) that which has been caught

560. PUERILE: (a) disgusting (b) nonsensical (c) childish (d) vulgar (e) perverse

561. FOIBLE: (a) idiosyncrasy (b) folly (c) weakness (d) mistake (e) fancy

562. TRAVESTY: (a) complete violation (b) gross misrepresentation (c) misinterpretation (d) grotesque imitation (e) shameless falsification

563. FACETIOUS: (a) unashamed (b) irreverent (c) arrogant (d) displaying levity (e) face-saving

564. TRAUMA: (a) uncontrollable behaviour (b) fits (c) temper tantrums (d) emotional shock (e) regressive behaviour

565. DIVERGENT: (a) parting ways (b) deviant (c) various (d) diversified (e) opposite

566. PULCHRITUDE: (a) fatness (b) beauty (c) tearfulness (d) greed (e) sensuality

567. MISDEMEANOUR: (a) misconduct (b) transgression (c) show of disrespect (d) offensive behaviour (e) discourtesy

554. (e)
555. (a)
556. (a)
557. (c)
558. (e)
559. (a)
560. (c)
561. (a)
562. (d)
563. (d)
564. (d)
565. (b)
566. (b)
567. (b)

568. BUCOLIC: (a) utopian (b) spirituous (c) pastoral (d) peaceful (e) noisy
569. MENDACIOUS: (a) begging (b) procrastinating (c) superficial (d) compromising (e) lying
570. FORTUITOUS: (a) lucky (b) courageous (c) appropriate (d) accidental (e) prompt
571. PAREGORIC: (a) pain-killer (b) cathartic (c) fever reducer (d) antiviral (e) emetic
572. DESULTORY: (a) dispirited (b) sad (c) abandoned (d) aimless (e) disconnected
573. NAIVETE (pronounced 'na-ive-tay'): (a) novelty (b) nativity (c) cleverness (d) ingenuousness (e) foolishness
574. ANIMADVERSION: (a) divagation (b) amplification (c) refutation (d) criticism (e) rejoinder
575. STYMIE: (a) stop (b) thwart (c) nullify (d) change direction (e) subvert
576. MISANTHROPE: (a) misadventurer (b) liar (c) miser (d) one who is in constant fear of disaster (e) one who hates mankind
577. FRENETIC: (a) insane (b) impatient (c) urgent (d) loud (e) frenzied
578. SEDULOUS: (a) assiduous (b) brilliant (c) smart (d) conscientious (e) cautious
579. COLOSSUS: (a) the statue of Julius Caesar (b) a monster (c) something very heavy (d) a mythical beast (e) a gigantic statue
580. BRAWN: (a) intellect (b) muscle (c) beef (d) salt water (e) military strength
581. OMINOUS: (a) foreboding evil (b) threatening (c) disastrous (d) unpleasant (e) unfavourable
582. DOUGHTY: (a) warlike (b) strong (c) well-built (d) fearless (e) courageous
583. FRACAS: (a) farce (b) brawl (c) confrontation (d) sweet smell (e) light breeze

568. (c)
569. (e)
570. (d)
571. (a)
572. (d)
573. (d)
574. (d)
575. (b)
576. (e)
577. (e)
578. (a)
579. (e)
580. (b)
581. (a)
582. (e)
583. (b)

584. METICULOUS: (a) methodical (b) hardworking (c) precise about details (d) strictly honest (e) thorough

585. PAROXYSM: (a) disaster (b) climax (c) delirium (d) fit (e) ecstasy

586. NASCENT: (a) incipient (b) inherent (c) potent (d) important (e) undying

587. MILIEU: (a) society (b) age (c) culture (d) environment (e) club

588. TENUOUS: (a) elastic (b) slender (c) flimsy (d) artificial (e) stubborn

589. EXTENUATING: (a) extending (b) complicating (c) lengthening (d) mitigating (e) proving guilt

590. FLEDGLING: (a) lackey (b) natural child (c) escapee (d) delicate (e) inexperienced

591. PEDANTIC: (a) scholarly (b) pedestrian (c) instructional (d) bookish (e) tedious

592. SKULDUGGERY: (a) using strong-arm methods (b) threatening (c) rank dishonesty (d) holding to ransom (e) trickery

593. CORPULENT: (a) lazy (b) greedy (c) over-sexed (d) deformed (e) fat

594. PARSIMONIUS: (a) careful (b) cautious (c) profligate (d) impartial (e) stingy

595. ADMONITION: (a) warning (b) fervent request (c) prohibition (d) disapproval (e) anger

596. MILLENNIUM: (a) 1,000,000 years (b) 100,000 years (c) 10,000 years (d) 1000 years (e) 50 centuries

597. MODICUM: (a) a trace (b) a large quantity (c) modesty (d) proper manners (e) etiquette

598. COMESTIBLE: (a) edible (b) beauty aids (c) sympathetic (d) easily inflammable (e) dispensable

599. REPREHENSIBLE: (a) blameworthy (b) cowardly (c) most unsatisfactory (d) responsible (e) vicious

584. (c)
585. (d)
586. (a)
587. (d)
588. (b)
589. (d)
590. (e)
591. (d)
592. (e)
593. (e)
594. (e)
595. (a)
596. (d)
597. (a)
598. (a)
599. (a)

600. JARGON: (a) slogan (b) specialized language (c) thieves' cant (d) slang (e) foreigner's speech
601. TEMPORAL: (a) lasting only for a time (b) worldly (c) secular (d) spiritual (e) of religion
602. COMPUNCTION: (a) remorse (b) pity (c) goodwill (d) compassion (e) hardheartedness
603. CORTEGE: (a) coffin (b) mourners (c) religious procession (d) funeral procession (e) pall bearers
604. KINETIC: (a) bovine (b) two-wheeled (c) flying (d) of motion (e) powerful
605. STILTED: (a) halting (b) trite (c) inclined (d) pompous (e) inadequately expressive
606. VERDANT: (a) sonorous (b) fragrant (c) green (d) well-wooded (e) fertile
607. FLIPPANT: (a) irreverent (b) unsteady (c) frolicsome (d) frivolous (e) casual
608. JINGOISM: (a) chauvinism (b) communalism (c) arrogant nationalism (d) separatism (e) world capitalism
609. GENRE: (a) category (b) general characteristics (c) superior class (d) significance (e) meaning
610. REPARTEE: (a) rejoinder (b) answer (c) witty reply (d) refutation (e) challenge
611. DISCOMFITED: (a) embarrassed (b) put into discomfort (c) proved wrong (d) disgraced (e) made uneasy
612. PENURIOUS: (a) parsimonious (b) painstaking (c) meticulous (d) extremely careful (e) rich
613. CARTE BLANCHE: (a) free pardon (b) blank cheque (c) credit card (d) unlimited authority (e) transit visa
614. WAGGISH: (a) facetious (b) oscillating (c) critical (d) vituperative (e) gossiping
615. JUNTA: (a) the underprivileged (b) the masses (c) power lords (d) the ruling power (e) military government

600. (b)
601. (d)
602. (a)
603. (d)
604. (d)
605. (d)
606. (c)
607. (d)
608. (a)
609. (a)
610. (c)
611. (a)
612. (a)
613. (d)
614. (a)
615. (e)

II

IS IT EXACTLY THE OPPOSITE?

In this section, out of the five choices which follow a headword, you have to pick out the one which is exactly its opposite. As said in the preceding section, a word may have more than one meaning; its antonym has to be chosen from the opposite of one of these meanings. To get these quizzes right, you must know, in the first instance, the *full* meaning of the headword. Once you know that accurately, finding the antonym will become an easy task. This will also explain why in this book the pride of place has been given to synonyms, and so many of them at that.

616. REDOLENT: (a) malodorous (b) cacophonous (c) stripped (d) aromatic (e) silent

617. REHEARSE: (a) redesign (b) recapitulate (c) repeat (d) forget (e) extemporize

618. QUALM: (a) twinge (b) remorse (c) compunction (d) restitution (e) relief

619. QUIESCENT: (a) agitated (b) disturbed (c) vexed (d) rejuvenated (e) nascent

620. CONTINGENT: (a) certain (b) uncertain (c) likely (d) unlikely (e) possible

621. IRASCIBLE: (a) tetchy (b) calm (c) sweet-tempered (d) benign (e) benevolent

622. RABBLE: (a) loyalist (b) clergy (c) aristocracy (d) philistine (e) populace

623. WAYWARD: (a) naughty (b) contrary (c) submissive (d) directional (e) astray

624. NONDESCRIPT: (a) identifiable (b) remarkable (c) prominent (d) distinguished (e) unclassified

625. OBFUSCATE: (a) rectify (b) clarify (c) explain (d) endorse (e) enlighten

626. OBNOXIOUS: (a) healthy (b) fragrant (c) lovable (d) pleasant (e) favourable

616. (a)
617. (e)
618. (e)
619. (a)
620. (d)
621. (b)
622. (c)
623. (c)
624. (a)
625. (b)
626. (d)

627. TART: (a) acid (b) sweet (c) quick (d) short (e) angry
628. SUPERNUMERARY: (a) inferior (b) essential (c) deficit (d) negligible (e) excessive
629. WAN: (a) spirited (b) florid (c) coarse (d) frigid (e) sprightly
630. PHLEGMATIC: (a) passionate (b) libidinous (c) erotic (d) impetuous (e) ardent
631. QUANDARY: (a) predicament (b) conquest (c) question (d) conviction (e) contradiction
632. WEIRD: (a) eerie (b) peculiar (c) familiar (d) magical (e) particular
633. SALUBRIOUS: (a) noxious (b) enervating (c) bracing (d) improper (e) unfriendly
634. PAUCITY: (a) interval (b) pause (c) abundance (d) dearth (e) defect
635. PECULATE: (a) be certain (b) surmise (c) pilfer (d) refund (e) economize
636. FRUMP: (a) slut (b) vagabond (c) unattractive woman (d) woman with uncombed hair (e) spirited, vulgar woman
637. VICARIOUS: (a) sinful (b) substitutional (c) perverse (d) self-experienced (e) denominational
638. NOTWITHSTANDING: (a) nevertheless (b) none the less (c) although (d) therefore (e) because
639. CRAVEN: (a) ardent (b) base (c) sycophantic (d) brave (e) importunate
640. OSTRACIZE: (a) import (b) admit (c) embrace (d) convert (e) reform
641. VINDICATE: (a) denounce (b) disregard (c) flout (d) castigate (e) flagellate
642. SEDULOUS: (a) truthful (b) unhealthy (c) lazy (d) unscholarly (e) uncaring
643. SENTENTIOUS: (a) wordy (b) abrupt (c) inflated (d) unkind (e) improper

627. (b)
628. (b)
629. (b)
630. (a)
631. (d)
632. (c)
633. (a)
634. (c)
635. (d)
636. (c)
637. (d)
638. (e)
639. (d)
640. (b)
641. (a)
642. (c)
643. (a)

644. PUSSILANIMOUS: (a) full of fighting spirit (b) cowardly (c) crafty (d) compromising (e) energetic
645. PERTINENT: (a) disrespectful (b) irrelevant (c) incorrect (d) misleading (e) deceptive
646. QUACK: (a) mountebank (b) dupe (c) gull (d) procurer (e) bizarre
647. HIATUS: (a) a conflict of opinions (b) bridge (c) contradiction (d) clash of interests (e) enmity
648. TENTATIVE: (a) provisional (b) experimental (c) on trial (d) final (e) ultimate
649. TRUCULENT: (a) gentle (b) confident (c) brave (d) untruthful (e) deceiving
650. PUNITIVE: (a) gigantic (b) rewarding (c) quick (d) unforgiving (e) mild
651. PROFANITY: (a) sacrilege (b) devotion (c) piety (d) rectitude (e) asceticism
652. BUXOM: (a) handsome (b) fat (c) flat-chested (d) attractive (e) sexy
653. COMPLAISANT: (a) disturbed (b) wrathful (c) wilful (d) indecisive (e) critical
654. CONCLAVE: (a) open assembly (b) meeting of heads of state (c) suburban township (d) pockets of foreign territory (e) protected place
655. CONSONANCE: (a) discord (b) accord (c) contradiction (d) sequence (e) consequence
656. EXHUME: (a) burn (b) bury (c) destroy (d) display (e) exhaust
657. VOUCHSAFE: (a) refuse (b) reject (c) deny (d) forswear (e) vilify
658. WHIMSICAL: (a) logical (b) reasonable (c) serious (d) wise (e) deliberating
659. PALPABLE: (a) mysterious (b) lost (c) immeasurable (d) doubtful (e) undesirable
660. WRANGLE: (a) contend (b) agree (c) submit (d) straighten (e) decipher

644. (a)
645. (b)
646. (b)
647. (b)
648. (d)
649. (a)
650. (b)
651. (c)
652. (c)
653. (c)
654. (a)
655. (a)
656. (b)
657. (a)
658. (c)
659. (d)
660. (b)

661. IRKSOME: (a) agreeable (b) cheerful (c) hilarious (d) tolerable (e) amiable
662. LIVID: (a) discoloured (b) bright (c) inflamed (d) animate (e) enraged
663. UNWONTED: (a) customary (b) prized (c) desirable (d) expected (e) welcomed
664. EXTANT: (a) scope (b) in existence (c) non-existent (d) archaic (e) outdated, but still in practice
665. BRAZEN: (a) modest (b) coated with brass (c) courageous (d) bright (e) shining
666. WITHER: (a) rejuvenate (b) hibernate (c) proliferate (d) disseminate (e) procrastinate
667. YOKEL: (a) peasant (b) gentleman (c) townsman (d) foreigner (e) bumpkin
668. PIQUE: (a) grudge (b) spite (c) umbrage (d) vex (e) pleasure
669. VULNERABLE: (a) open (b) sinless (c) infallible (d) protected (e) defended
670. RETICENT: (a) vocal (b) wrongful (c) irregular (d) communicative (e) clamorous
671. MERETRICIOUS: (a) disgraceful (b) stupid (c) gaudy (d) common (e) plain
672. FACTITIOUS: (a) joking at inappropriate times (b) genuine (c) tendency to break away and form factions (d) quarrelsome (e) artificial
673. HALCYON: (a) ideal (b) mythical (c) magical (d) calm (e) stormy
674. LIMPID: (a) pure (b) transparent (c) free from defilement (d) muddy (e) clear
675. ZEALOUS: (a) ardent (b) apathetic (c) eager (d) enthusiastic (e) envious
676. ENCOMIUM: (a) salary (b) eulogy (c) excellence (d) criticism (e) abuse
677. DEMURE: (a) self-satisfied (b) flirtatious (c) modest (d) shy (e) pretty
678. COVERT: (a) open (b) conspiring (c) straightforward (d) daring (e) secret

661. (a)
662. (b)
663. (a)
664. (c)
665. (a)
666. (a)
667. (c)
668. (e)
669. (d)
670. (d)
671. (e)
672. (b)
673. (e)
674. (d)
675. (b)
676. (d)
677. (b)
678. (a)

679. RUEFULLY: (a) amicably (b) calmly (c) quickly (d) without regret (e) willingly

680. DECIDUOUS: (a) bearing fruit twice in a year (b) seeds with two segments (c) deciding judiciously (d) shedding leaves annually (e) evergreen

681. EMEND: (a) repair (b) correct (c) improve (d) cure (e) introduce mistakes

682. PROTRUDE: (a) intrude (b) obtrude (c) extrude (d) recede (e) concede

683. WAG: (a) critic (b) skunk (c) wit (d) dullard (e) wayward

684. CLEAVE: (a) join (b) strike (c) split (d) embrace (e) stitching up

685. PLASTIC: (a) ferrous (b) ductile (c) rigid (d) intractable (e) wooden

686. SUAVE: (a) bland (b) rough (c) mollifying (d) crude (e) polite

687. TRANSGRESS: (a) observe (b) obey (c) transfer (d) violate (e) transmit

688. SYBARITE: (a) ascetic (b) sadist (c) nymphomaniac (d) hedonistic (e) puritanical

689. HUBRIS: (a) hooded terror (b) humility (c) pride (d) incontinence (e) anger

690. CATACHRESIS: (a) crisis management (b) ability to concentrate (c) correct use of words (d) forgetfulness (e) loss of memory

691. INNOCUOUS: (a) infertile (b) harmful (c) innocent (d) erroneous (e) bland

692. PACIFIC: (a) martial (b) arrogant (c) fractious (d) violent (e) Atlantic

693. OVERWROUGHT: (a) indifferent (b) stoical (c) calm (d) idle (e) cheerful

694. TIMOROUS: (a) frightened (b) courageous (c) hesitant (d) diffident (e) strong

695. SMUG: (a) uncomfortable (b) unpleasant (c) clear (d) self-critical (e) sentimental

679. (b)
680. (e)
681. (e)
682. (d)
683. (d)
684. (a)
685. (c)
686. (b)
687. (a)
688. (a)
689. (b)
690. (c)
691. (b)
692. (d)
693. (c)
694. (b)
695. (d)

696. NUNNERY: (a) monastery (b) cloister (c) priory (d) bordello (e) hospice
697. PROVIDENT: (a) pensionable (b) prodigal (c) irresponsible (d) careful (e) unscrupulous
698. SPLENETIC: (a) calm (b) casual (c) genial (d) restrained (e) moderate
699. THRESHOLD: (a) exit (b) end (c) implemented (d) entrance (e) release
700. SPORADIC: (a) scattered (b) violent (c) every now and then (d) localized (e) accidental
701. HAGIOGRAPHY: (a) order of saints (b) biography of saints (c) worship of inanimate objects (d) uncritical praise (e) biography of sinners
702. REPROBATION: (a) suspended sentence (b) warning (c) censure (d) approval (e) recommendation
703. FECUNDITY: (a) profusion (b) fertility (c) shortage (d) potentiality (e) barrenness
704. TICKLISH: (a) titillating (b) irritating (c) easy (d) critical (e) pleasant
705. SCOURGE: (a) pacify (b) please (c) pamper (d) reward (e) denigrate
706. TANTAMOUNT: (a) approximate (b) equivalent (c) loss (d) unequal (e) synonymous
707. PROPITIATE: (a) anger (b) annoy (c) oppose (d) condemn (e) defy
708. PELLUCID: (a) opaque (b) translucent (c) pale (d) bright (e) ethereal
709. SALACIOUS: (a) prurient (b) puritanical (c) calm (d) chaste (e) wise
710. SANG-FROID: (a) savoir-faire (b) anxiety (c) excitability (d) involvement (e) complication
711. QUIXOTIC: (a) mad (b) romantic (c) realistic (d) visionary (e) predictable
712. PUTATIVE: (a) ascribed (b) original (c) legal (d) actual (e) married

696. (d)
697. (b)
698. (c)
699. (b)
700. (d)
701. (e)
702. (e)
703. (e)
704. (c)
705. (c)
706. (d)
707. (a)
708. (a)
709. (d)
710. (c)
711. (c)
712. (d)

713. ARRAIGN: (a) extol (b) abuse (c) plead (d) condemn (e) excuse
714. WANTON: (a) modest (b) disciplined (c) rational (d) abstemious (e) temperate
715. PROLIX: (a) clever (b) punctual (c) charitable (d) precise (e) smart
716. SUCCULENT: (a) dry (b) tough (c) unappetizing (d) unhelpful (e) indigestible
717. RETRIBUTION: (a) reprisal (b) compensation (c) amelioration (d) exaction (e) pardon
718. SURMOUNT: (a) submit (b) surpass (c) subjugate (d) support (e) subserve
719. SUPPLICATE: (a) deny (b) implicate (c) assert (d) demand (e) insult
720. SURLY: (a) genial (b) cheerful (c) gay (d) playful (e) demure
721. PERFUNCTORY: (a) quick (b) careless (c) thorough (d) final (e) arrogant
722. PERNICIOUS: (a) baneful (b) benign (c) baleful (d) humorous (e) harmless
723. COALESCE: (a) divide (b) become sticky (c) form a government (d) unite diverse interests (e) form a pattern
724. PRAGMATIC: (a) according to reason (b) practical (c) theoretical (d) absolute (e) provisional
725. PRIM: (a) lugubrious (b) informal (c) solvenly (d) prissy (e) vulgar
726. SACRILEGIOUS: (a) pious (b) sacred (c) scandalous (d) impious (e) iconoclastic
727. RELEGATE: (a) entrust (b) abdicate (c) promote (d) surrender (e) demote
728. UNREMITTING: (a) pardoning (b) assiduous (c) faithful (d) inconstant (e) faltering
729. UNSULLIED: (a) affected (b) satisfied (c) hurried (d) disgraced (e) tarnished
730. EXULT: (a) glorify (b) extol (c) bemoan (d) vilify (e) rejoice

713. (a)
714. (a)
715. (d)
716. (a)
717. (e)
718. (a)
719. (d)
720. (a)
721. (c)
722. (e)
723. (a)
724. (c)
725. (e)
726. (a)
727. (c)
728. (d)
729. (e)
730. (c)

731. ZENITH: (a) vortex (b) apex (c) vertex (d) nadir (e) antipodes
732. ZEST: (a) laziness (b) gusto (c) distaste (d) ill-health (e) animosity
733. PERFIDY: (a) loyalty (b) truthfulness (c) trust (d) rebellion (e) treachery
734. AQUILINE: (a) perfectly straight (b) slightly upturned (c) crooked (d) symmetrical (e) hooked
735. VENIAL: (a) sinful (b) unforgivable (c) corrupt (d) arrogant (e) gentle
736. VERACIOUS: (a) hungry (b) frugal (c) false (d) undependable (e) gentle
737. BLATANT: (a) shameless (b) indirect (c) clever (d) aggressive (e) deceptive
738. TURBULENT: (a) tumultuous (b) exciting (c) fading (d) calm (e) friendly
739. ATTENUATE: (a) to rectify (b) to excuse (c) to strengthen (d) to weaken (e) to improve
740. BEDRAGGLED: (a) defeated (b) wearing torn clothes (c) weary (d) undisciplined (e) dry
741. BELIE: (a) suggest (b) confirm (c) fail to satisfy (d) lie underneath (e) disappoint
742. WRATHFUL: (a) choleric (b) phlegmatic (c) happy (d) revengeful (e) serene
743. WRY: (a) straight (b) open (c) guileless (d) easy (e) tortuous
744. SQUEAMISH: (a) licentious (b) punctilious (c) scrupulous (d) uncomplaining (e) indifferent
745. PROSCRIBE: (a) prescribe (b) commend (c) classify (d) prohibit (e) embrace
746. VOLUPTUARY: (a) hedonist (b) ascetic (c) reclusive (d) masochistic (e) unattractive
747. RESTIVE: (a) obedient (b) unassuming (c) alert (d) ceaseless (e) energetic
748. SCEPTIC: (a) incredulous (b) optimistic (c) generous (d) zealot (e) companionable

731. (d)
732. (c)
733. (a)
734. (a)
735. (b)
736. (c)
737. (b)
738. (d)
739. (c)
740. (e)
741. (b)
742. (e)
743. (a)
744. (e)
745. (a)
746. (b)
747. (a)
748. (d)

749. REMONSTRATE: (a) allow (b) forget (c) protest (d) accept (e) disprove

750. ENDEMIC: (a) conclusive (b) localized (c) widespread (d) virulent (e) contagious

751. ENERVATE: (a) invigorate (b) soothe (c) weaken (d) deplete (e) augment

752. INURED: (a) bored (b) protected (c) unaccustomed (d) secure (e) accustomed

753. ABSTEMIOUS: (a) teetotal (b) economical (c) self-indulgent (d) temperate (e) abstinent

754. ADMONISH: (a) warn (b) pledge (c) detain (d) threaten (e) encourage

755. WARILY: (a) negligently (b) timidly (c) vigilantly (d) noisily (e) circumstantially

756. LAMBENT: (a) impending (b) subdued (c) steady (d) bright (e) flickering

757. LIMBO: (a) place for the forgotten (b) coma (c) dreadful place (d) paradise (e) dullness

758. INIQUITY: (a) honesty (b) impartiality (c) mercy (d) righteousness (e) charity

759. INNATE: (a) congenital (b) natural (c) acquired (d) promoted (e) sophisticated

760. WILY: (a) youthful (b) articulate (c) stout (d) straightforward (e) stupid

761. PERDITION: (a) state of grace (b) great danger (c) pardoning (d) damnation (e) predicament

762. ADROIT: (a) successful (b) quick (c) inept (d) bold (e) courageous

763. ABSTRUSE: (a) clear (b) abstract (c) difficult to understand (d) philosophical (e) of high quality

764. ABROGATE: (a) violate (b) enforce (c) break (d) change (e) modify

765. DISINGENUOUS: (a) calculating (b) frank (c) complex (d) unconvincing (e) honest

749. (d)
750. (c)
751. (a)
752. (c)
753. (c)
754. (e)
755. (a)
756. (c)
757. (d)
758. (d)
759. (c)
760. (d)
761. (c)
762. (c)
763. (a)
764. (b)
765. (b)

766. CHAUVINISM: (a) aggressiveness (b) contempt for women (c) wife-beating (d) internationalism (e) readiness to fight for the country
767. STAUNCH: (a) wavering (b) corrupt (c) immoral (d) untrustworthy (e) unfaithful
768. STILTED: (a) straight (b) simple (c) uncomplicated (d) poetic (e) sublime
769. DIFFIDENCE: (a) false confidence (b) lack of courage (c) hesitation (d) confidence (e) overconfidence
770. UNFEIGNED: (a) genuine (b) pretended (c) justifiable (d) original (e) reconciled
771. BIGOTED: (a) superstitious (b) arrogant (c) tolerant (d) prejudiced (e) wrongheaded
772. TANGIBLE: (a) palpable (b) abstract (c) illusory (d) impossible (e) possible
773. INFERNAL: (a) fertile (b) diabolical (c) atheistic (d) known (e) heavenly
774. BLAND: (a) unsalted (b) mild (c) easily digested (d) harmless (e) tasty
775. INGENIOUS: (a) artful (b) guilty (c) unskilful (d) dishonest (e) insincere
776. VICISSITUDE: (a) benevolence (b) stability (c) saintliness (d) harmlessness (e) dependability
777. PROMISCUOUS: (a) secretive (b) holding great promise (c) chaste (d) mixed up (e) sexually irregular
778. PROPITIOUS: (a) bad (b) untimely (c) premature (d) unfavourable (e) unlucky
779. RIFE: (a) common (b) numerous (c) prevalent (d) scarce (e) unready
780. IRREVOCABLE: (a) stoppable (b) capable of solution (c) capable of withdrawal (d) capable of amendment (e) alterable
781. REPLETE: (a) deplete (b) satiated (c) abounding (d) empty (e) decimated

766. (d)
767. (e)
768. (b)
769. (d)
770. (b)
771. (c)
772. (b)
773. (e)
774. (e)
775. (c)
776. (b)
777. (c)
778. (d)
779. (d)
780. (e)
781. (d)

782. INVIDIOUS: (a) callous (b) just (c) kind (d) impartial (e) discriminatory
783. OPIATE: (a) anodyne (b) stimulant (c) deodorant (d) irritant (e) abrasive
784. DOLDRUMS: (a) stagnation (b) intense activity (c) turmoil (d) disorganization (e) insecurity
785. EGREGIOUS: (a) one who moves from woman to woman (b) nomadic (c) sticking close together (d) extremely distinguished (e) outstandingly good
786. PROFLIGATE: (a) economical (b) abstemious (c) puritanical (d) virtuous (e) generous
787. TRIBULATION: (a) confidence (b) happiness (c) success (d) celebration (e) rancour
788. METTLESOME: (a) non-interesting (b) placid (c) friendly (d) cowardly (e) ferocious
789. MINDLESS: (a) intelligent (b) careful (c) witty (d) astute (e) talented
790. MISCHANCE: (a) chance (b) accident (c) disaster (d) luck (e) prosperity
791. MODISH: (a) vulgar (b) unfashionable (c) shabby (d) immodest (e) genteel
792. IMPREGNABLE: (a) that which cannot be penetrated (b) that which can be penetrated (c) fecund (d) infertile (e) very strong
793. JADE: (a) fag (b) exhaust (c) quicken (d) strengthen (e) revive
794. JAUNTY: (a) sad (b) serious (c) careful (d) deferential (e) slow
795. JEOPARDY: (a) victory (b) triumph (c) predicament (d) solution (e) safety
796. JUDICIOUS: (a) unjust (b) indiscreet (c) clumsy (d) mindless (e) uncircumspect
797. LACONIC: (a) polite (b) uninterested (c) hostile (d) loquacious (e) informal
798. EXIGENCY: (a) grave situation (b) normalcy (c) unsettled condition (d) expediency (e) possible condition

782. (b)
783. (b)
784. (b)
785. (e)
786. (d)
787. (b)
788. (d)
789. (b)
790. (d)
791. (b)
792. (b)
793. (e)
794. (b)
795. (e)
796. (b)
797. (d)
798. (b)

799. PROPENSITY: (a) penchant (b) proclivity (c) design (d) density (e) disinclination
800. EMPIRICAL: (a) based on logic (b) based on theory (c) based on instinct (d) based on experience (e) based on knowledge
801. MOLLIFY: (a) discipline (b) provoke (c) pamper (d) persuade (e) deny
802. NICETY: (a) discourtesy (b) rudeness (c) carelessness (d) impropriety (e) indiscretion
803. PURGE: (a) deterge (b) instal (c) glorify (d) deify (e) pollute
804. PLATONIC: (a) friendly (b) sensual (c) unfulfilled love (d) devoted (e) spiritual
805. PONDEROUS: (a) light (b) straightforward (c) simplified (d) precise (e) clear
806. PRACTISED: (a) unskilled (b) neglected (c) clumsy (d) nervous (e) amateurish
807. RAPACIOUS: (a) chaste (b) friendly (c) generous (d) well behaved (e) slow
808. BRUSQUE: (a) harsh (b) quick (c) unkind (d) rude (e) polite
809. BUMPTIOUS: (a) humble (b) rowdy (c) polite (d) unmannerly (e) high-spirited
810. OBTUSE: (a) clear (b) fast (c) sharp (d) stolid (e) reliable
811. ODIUM: (a) sympathy (b) love (c) friendship (d) comradeship (e) brotherhood
812. ONUS: (a) irresponsibility (b) innocence (c) stigma (d) neglect (e) relief
813. UNEQUIVOCAL: (a) false (b) ambiguous (c) straightforward (d) quibbling (e) hesitant
814. COGNOMEN: (a) family name (b) first name (c) capacity to understand (d) assumed name (e) significance
815. ASPERITY: (a) impatience (b) cheerfulness (c) sharpness of intellect (d) bitterness (e) accusation

113

799. (e)
800. (b)
801. (b)
802. (c)
803. (e)
804. (b)
805. (a)
806. (a)
807. (c)
808. (e)
809. (a)
810. (c)
811. (b)
812. (e)
813. (b)
814. (d)
815. (b)

816. EXONERATE: (a) excuse (b) acquit (c) implicate (d) examine (e) condemn
817. TOUCHY: (a) fretful (b) refractory (c) sensitive (d) affable (e) peevish
818. TREPIDATION: (a) confidence (b) courage (c) mirth (d) delay (e) calmness
819. INGENUOUS: (a) naive (b) clever (c) mechanical (d) complicated (e) new
820. INHIBITION: (a) release (b) recklessness (c) licentiousness (d) ardour (e) prohibition
821. TOOTHSOME: (a) unsavoury (b) sour (c) liquid (d) predigested (e) palatable
822. TORPID: (a) cold (b) temperate (c) indolent (d) motionless (e) active
823. ABEYANCE: (a) setting aside (b) rejection (c) suspension (d) implementation (e) inactivity
824. CALLOW: (a) green (b) clumsy (c) experienced (d) countrified (e) immature
825. CASUISTRY: (a) philosophical dispute (b) religious disputation (c) act of bad faith (d) tiresome argument (e) clear reasoning
826. PERSECUTE: (a) discontinue (b) neglect (c) hunt (d) assist (e) befriend
827. VITUPERATION: (a) worship (b) devotion (c) malignity (d) praise (e) construction
828. SEDUCTIVE: (a) chaste (b) puritanical (c) horrific (d) enticing (e) repulsive
829. INDUCE: (a) force (b) persuade (c) distract (d) prohibit (e) discourage
830. TETCHY: (a) crooked (b) honest (c) kind (d) insensitive (e) good-natured
831. TENEBROUS: (a) resplendent (b) clear (c) steady (d) dependable (e) strong
832. CACOPHONY: (a) loud noise (b) symphony (c) chatter (d) voices in many languages (e) band of wind instruments
833. PERSPICUOUS: (a) dry (b) easy (c) lucid (d) obscure (e) outlandish

816. (c)
817. (d)
818. (e)
819. (b)
820. (a)
821. (a)
822. (e)
823. (d)
824. (c)
825. (e)
826. (e)
827. (d)
828. (e)
829. (e)
830. (e)
831. (a)
832. (b)
833. (d)

834. INEBRIATED: (a) released (b) celebrated (c) sorrowful (d) sober (e) capable
835. INFAMY: (a) prominence (b) reputation (c) honesty (d) sobriety (e) immortality
836. LOATH: (a) eager (b) agreeable (c) loving (d) hostile (e) attracted
837. CORPOREAL: (a) collective (b) concerning public corporations (c) material (d) spiritual (e) divine
838. BOISTEROUS: (a) violent (b) offensive (c) quiet (d) merry (e) unruly
839. CHARY: (a) quick (b) reluctant (c) suspicious (d) incautious (e) nervous
840. ASSIDUOUS: (a) dull (b) lazy (c) methodical (d) untiring (e) hard-working
841. VOCIFEROUS: (a) objectionable (b) violent (c) self-restrained (d) silent (e) meditative
842. OBSOLETE: (a) old-fashioned (b) obscure (c) obsolescent (d) up-to-date (e) rejected
843. TORTUOUS: (a) harsh (b) pitiless (c) straight (d) kind (e) merciful

III
HOW WELL DO YOU SPELL ?

Two or more spellings are given for each word. Identify the correct one. Although both British and American spellings are perfectly valid, one can't mix the two styles in one's writing, which is what happens quite often. For the purposes of this book, only the British spellings are the correct choice, as the teaching of English in India follows the British practice. If you make one spelling mistake in a year and learn to rectify it, you are not a bad speller.

844. (a) paralleled (b) paralelled (c) parallelled
845. (a) villify (b) vilify
846. (a) resistance (b) resistence

834. (d)
835. (b)
836. (a)
837. (d)
838. (c)
839. (d)
840. (b)
841. (d)
842. (d)
843. (c)
844. (a)
845. (b)
846. (a)

847. (a) acommodate (b) accommodate (c) accomodate
848. (a) niece (b) neice
849. (a) fullfilment (b) fulfilment (c) fulfillment
850. (a) harassment (b) harrassment (c) harrasment
851. (a) embarassment (b) embarrassment (c) embarrasment
852. (a) tranquillity (b) tranquility
853. (a) concieve (b) conceive
854. (a) recieve (b) receive
855. (a) deceive (b) decieve
856. (a) acquiesce (b) acquiese (c) acqeisce
857. (a) apalling (b) appalling (c) appaling
858. (a) irresistible (b) irrestable
859. (a) seperate (b) separate
860. (a) indispensible (b) indispensable
861. In the sense of unmoving: (a) stationary (b) stationery
862. (a) resemblence (b) resemblance
863. (a) succession (b) succesion
864. (a) successful (b) succesfull (c) succeful
865. (a) rhythm (b) rythm
866. (a) persevere (b) persever
867. (a) wierd (b) weird
868. (a) targetted (b) targeted
869. (a) reminise (b) reminisce
870. (a) hygiene (b) hygeine
871. (a) siezure (b) seizure
872. (a) siege (b) seige
873. (a) consceintious (b) conscientious (c) conscientous
874. (a) languor (b) langour
875. (a) exentric (b) ecstentric (c) eccentric
876. (a) dilettante (b) dilletante
877. (a) laison (b) liaison (c) laiason
878. (a) budgetted (b) budgeted
879. (a) amanuesis (b) amanuensis
880. (a) horripillation (b) horripilation

119

847. (b)
848. (a)
849. (b)
850. (a)
851. (b)
852. (a)
853. (b)
854. (b)
855. (a)
856. (a)
857. (b)
858. (a)
859. (b)
860. (b)
861. (a)
862. (b)
863. (a)
864. (a)
865. (a)
866. (a)
867. (b)
868. (b)
869. (b)
870. (a)
871. (b)
872. (a)
873. (b)
874. (a)
875. (c)
876. (a)
877. (b)
878. (b)
879. (b)
880. (b)

881. (a) collossal (b) colossal (c) collosal
882. (a) corollary (b) corrollary (c) corrolary
883. (a) correlation (b) corelation (c) correllation
884. (a) supersede (b) supercede (c) superseed
885. (a) independant (b) independent
886. (a) xerox (b) zerox
887. (a) concensus (b) consensus
888. (a) advertize (b) advertise
889. (a) worshiping (b) worshipping
890. (a) benefited (b) benefitted
891. (a) criticige (b) criticise
892. (a) sceptic (b) skeptic (c) skeptik
893. (a) deciduous (b) decidious
894. (a) diaphonous (b) diaphanous
895. (a) exuberence (b) exuberance
896. (a) tolerent (b) tolerant
897. (a) analyze (b) analyse
898. (a) obsequeous (b) obsequious
899. (a) pretence (b) pretense
900. (a) sychophantic (b) sycophantic
901. (a) ressurection (b) resurrection (c) ressurrec-
     tion
902. (a)   diarrhoea   (b)   diahrroea   (c)   diarria
     (d) diahrroea
903. (a) abcess (b) absess (c) abscess (d) absces
904. (a) aquittal (b) acquital (c) acquittal

IV

HAVE YOU GOT THE RIGHT WORD ?

Words with a similar sound or words with near-similar
sounds, words with slightly different spellings, and
near synonyms with different nuances of meaning
have been called 'lexicographical nightmares', as even
people who speak and write good English sometimes
confuse them. Here are some you should be careful
about. The test sentences have been taken from *Collins*

881. (b)
882. (a)
883. (a)
884. (a)
885. (b)
886. (a)
887. (b)
888. (b)
889. (b)
890. (a)
891. (b)
892. (a)
893. (a)
894. (a)
895. (b)
896. (b)
897. (b)
898. (b)
899. (a)
900. (b)
901. (b)
902. (a)
903. (c)
904. (c)

COBUILD English Language Dictionary, which gives actual contemporary usage.

905. How can you approve of the —— sport of hunting?
    (a) barbaric (b) barbarous

906. —— between the two sides in this dispute will be a delicate business.
    (a) Arbitrating (b) Mediating

907. Her undisputed good looks caused —— and admiration.
    (a) covetousness (b) envy (c) jealousy

908. A faint, sweet, woody —— hung in the air.
    (a) odour (b) aroma (c) scent

909. She —— a smile.
    (a) assayed (b) essayed

910. A lexicographer was once kissing his maid, when suddenly the wife entered the room. 'Why, N, I'm —— (1)', she said. 'Madam', the lexicographer said, '*I'm* —— (1), you are —— (2)'. Of the two words, surprised and astonished, which is (1) and which is (2)?

911. She will —— herself on those who helped him to escape.
    (a) revenge (b) avenge

912. We saw his —— eyes fixed on us.
    (a) baleful (b) baneful

913. They paid 28% above market —— for it.
    (a) cost (b) price (c) value

914. Traders and artisans do not constitute a —— in the strict sense.
    (a) bourgeois (b) bourgeoise (c) bourgeoisie

915. Do you want a —— ?
    (a) cacao (b) cocoa (c) coca (d) coco

916. The Kirks are ə —— couple, and believe in dividing all tasks equally.
    (a) contemporary (b) modern

917. —— I have a word with you, please?
    (a) Can (b) May

123

905. (a)
906. (b)
907. (b)
908. (a)
909. (b)
910. (1) surprised (2) astonished
911. (a)
912. (a)
913. (c)
914. (c)
915. (b)
916. (b)
917. (b)

918. It was sad to see her the victim of — pain.
(a) continual (b) continuous

919. A strange new society is apparently — in our midst.
(a) erupting (b) irrupting

920. Life is a — pain.
(a) continual (b) continuous

921. He laughed —, even holding his sides.
(a) exceedingly (b) excessively

922. By bribing her, I won — to some files.
(a) access (b) accession

923. You are showing a — lack of courage.
(a) contemptuous (b) contemptible

924. Through a combination of —, the meeting was a failure.
(a) accidents (b) mishaps

925. If a set of ideas —, it leads to a satisfactory conclusion.
(a) coheres (b) adheres

926. It would be better to close our eyes like a — husband whose wife has taken a lover.
(a) complacent (b) complaisant

927. With the — of old age he lost some of his enthusiasm for life.
(a) advance (b) advancement

928. Most towns had taken some — precautions of a civil defence nature.
(a) elemental (b) elementary

929. He didn't have an — in the world.
(a) adversary (b) antagonist (c) enemy (d) foe
(e) opponent

930. Most people protect themselves from — to their self-esteem.
(a) damage (b) injury

931. A week later, read the meter again and — the first reading from the second.
(a) deduct (b) subtract

932. He couldn't spell, which particularly — her.
(a) aggravated (b) annoyed (c) irritated

918. (a)
919. (a)
920. (a)
921. (b)
922. (a)
923. (b)
924. (b)
925. (a)
926. (b)
927. (a)
928. (b)
929. (c)
930. (b)
931. (b)
932. (b)

933. Americans are — about the whole business of royalty.
(a) ambiguous (b) ambivalent
934. The English public schools are an —
(a) anachronism (b) anomaly
935. She came — into the room.
(a) flying (b) fleeing
936. Nuclear energy is dangerous and —.
(a) amoral (b) immoral
937. His lawyer had been — him again not to answer questions.
(a) abjuring (b) adjuring
938. I finished the journey — refreshed.
(a) positively (b) absolutely
939. He resigned with — timing.
(a) masterly (b) masterful
940. ... a fairly flat plateau at an — of about a hundred feet.
(a) altitude (b) elevation
941. There was nothing — in the message thumped out in his newspaper articles.
(a) ambiguous (b) equivocal
942. In the case of countries belonging to the EEC, their social security system is linked to Britain by a — agreement.
(a) mutual (b) reciprocal
943. The citizens of Massachusetts voted yes in a — to cut property tax.
(a) plebiscite (b) referendum
944. The bedroom was simple but —.
(a) tasteful (b) tasty
945. He likes wearing — hats.
(a) comic (b) comical
946. Given his liking for —, he might well have added that, if a job was worth doing, it was worth doing well.
(a) commonplace (b) truism (c) platitude

933. (b)
934. (a)
935. (a)
936. (b)
937. (b)
938. (a)
939. (b)
940. (b)
941. (a)
942. (b)
943. (b)
944. (a)
945. (a)
946. (c)

947. The broadcast — with a close-up film of babies crying.
(a) began (b) started

948. ... the — between peace and war.
(a) alternative (b) choice

949. The only permanent water supply was — the ground.
(a) below (b) under

950. I wrote — letters home, telling everyone how I was progressing.
(a) cheerful (b) cheery

951. Authoritarian rulers are typically — and capricious.
(a) venal (b) venial

952. The new legislation, —, will lead to some improvements.
(a) hopefully (b) we hope

953. ... a real desire to modernise Britain and free it from — tradition...
(a) ancient (b) antiquated

954. The financial markets had raised interest rates in — of a squeeze.
(a) anticipation (b) expectation

955. I have already — the interest that has been shown.
(a) alluded to (b) eluded

V

ESOTERIC WORDS

These words do not belong to any cult engaged in mysterious rites; these are called esoteric because only a few would feel comfortable using them, and only a handful of readers would get their precise meaning without having recourse to a dictionary. Read, for instance, Saul Bellow's recent novel, *More Die of Heartbreak*, and see how many uncommon words you

947. (a)
948. (b)
949. (a)
950. (a)
951. (a)
952. (b)
953. (b)
954. (a)
955. (a)

come across. Who knows when you may need to use these words yourself; so jump into the fray, and good luck.

956. FIBRIL: (a) fibrous (b) root of hair (c) frilly dress (d) torn fibre (e) feverish

957. RUBRIC: (a) ceremonial dress (b) title page of a book (c) rules of conduct (d) initiation ceremony (e) introduction

958. AEROBICAL: (a) concerning air (b) aerial acrobatics (c) aeronotical (d) subsisting on oxygen (e) of airborne germs

959. ATRIUM: (a) revenge (b) entrance of a building (c) room in which clerical vestments are kept (d) the lower chamber of each half of the heart (e) open main court of a Roman house

960. MORPHOLOGY: (a) study of the development and form of organisms (b) study of speech elements having a meaning (c) study of the addictive drugs (d) study of the evolutionary development of living forms (e) study of the form and structure of words

961. PRIMIPARA: (a) the firstborn (b) an only child (c) a person who has just been initiated (d) the opening paragraph of a book or essay (e) a woman who has borne only one child

962. CROTCHETS: (a) clutches (b) small parts of maches (c) hooklike device (d) the part of trousers where the genitals rest (e) forked sticks

963. FINAGLING: (a) using trickery on a person (b) fishing for compliments (c) looking for faults (d) embezzling (e) paying too much attention to another's husband or wife

964. MANTIC: (a) with a long body like a mantis (b) crazed (c) psychopathic killer (d) having prophetic powers (e) Spanish cloak

965. IRREFRAGABLE: (a) indisputable (b) unbreakable (c) inviolable (d) intractable (e) indispensable

956. (b)
957. (c)
958. (d)
959. (e)
960. (e)
961. (e); for no child the word is nullipara
962. (c)
963. (a)
964. (d)
965. (a)

966. KLEPTOCRAT: (a) employer of thieves (b) leader of a thieves' gang (c) belonging to the class of compulsive thieves (d) someone who cuts other people's pockets, i.e., taxman (e) shop detective

967. ODOMETER: (a) a device to measure smell (b) a device to measure the level of water (c) a device to test the firmness of teeth (d) milometer (e) postage meter

968. PATCHOULI: (a) ladies' purse (b) ladies' underwear (c) cheap perfume (d) a kind of heavy perfume (e) an aphrodisiac

969. OSTEOPOROSIS: (a) brittleness of bones (b) benign tumour composed of bone tissues (c) leaking bone marrow (d) chronic inflammation of the bone joints (e) softening of the bones

970. TERGIVERSATE: (a) hesitate (b) change loyalties (c) make excuses (d) contradict (e) play for time

971. ARRHYTHMIC: (a) characterized by periodic stoppage (b) verses which do not scan properly (c) characterized by irregular heartbeat (d) suffering from heart failure (e) breathing which is spasmodic

972. SOMATOLOGY: (a) study of the structure and function of the body (b) study of the life cycle of diseases (c) study of micro-organisms (d) study of abnormal psyche (e) study of the human body's immunity system

973. GERRYMANDER (pronounced 'jerry-'): (a) forcibly occupy civilian property (b) to use strong-arm tactics to secure votes (c) divide polling constituency to one's advantage (d) to lobby with powerful nations to start a war (e) to sell excess stock at throwaway prices

974. AFFECTS: (a) influences (b) personal belongings (c) property left by the deceased (d) emotions associated with an idea (e) false airs

966. (c)
967. (d)
968. (d)
969. (a)
970. (b)
971. (c)
972. (a)
973. (c)
974. (d)

975. VERMICULAR: (a) having the property of destroying worms (b) made of vermicelli (c) relating to worms (d) resembling worms (e) with very fine strands

976. IDIOMORPHIC: (a) relating to the study of individuals (b) relating to any disease of unknown cause (c) plant cell differing from those around it in the same tissue (d) minerals occurring naturally in the form of well-developed crystals (e) relating to the particular variety of language used by any social group

977. RAUNCHY: (a) feisty (b) lecherous (c) irritable (d) rough (e) full of energy

978. POMOLOGIST: (a) a critic of poetry (b) an expert sword player (c) a pisciculture expert (d) an expert on the grafting of roses (e) a fruit cultivation expert

979. WAFTAGE: (a) wordiness in speech (b) price charged for transportation (c) the draught of a ship (d) waste matter in the process of production (e) buoyant conveyance

980. EYETEETH: (a) upper canines (b) wisdom teeth (c) teeth of a comb (d) small holes in dresses for insertion of hooks (e) acts of great sacrifice

981. DEMIURGE: (a) a woman with a bad repute (b) one who is part mortal part god (c) a large bottle with a short narrow neck (d) feeble desire (e) creator of the universe

982. THANATOS: (a) personification of death (b) personification of thunder (c) lord of the flies (d) personification of retribution (e) lord of the nether worlds

983. DAEMON: (a) the Devil (b) the guardian spirit (c) bad angel (d) a temper (e) the spirit of revenge

135

975. (c)
976. (d)
977. (b)
978. (e)
979. (e)
980. (a)
981. (e)
982. (a)
983. (b)

984. **DOLICHOCEPHALIC:** (a) containing coarse-grained basalt (b) given to uncontrollable grief (c) shaped like a hatchet (d) a head much longer than it is broad (e) having a medium-sized head

985. **VAMPY:** (a) seductive (b) gypsy-like (c) a woman who leaves men in a state of wreck (d) sluttish (e) an elusive woman

986. **VULCANISM:** (a) processes that result in the formation of volcanoes (b) the tendency to erupt, particularly as a result of emotional stress (c) the tendency to change rapidly from a solid to a liquid state (d) treating natural rubber with sulphur to make it hard (e) follow the cult of Vulcan, the fire-god

987. **HOMONGOUS:** (a) of only one colour (b) monstrously large (c) similar in structure or parts because of common ancestry (d) words having the same spelling but different meanings (e) self-fertilizing

988. **DISCOMBOBULATED:** (a) made uneasy (b) disentangled (c) made easy (d) thrown into confusion (e) inconvenienced

The preceding thirty-three items in this section were not hand-picked for your exasperation; they are all from Saul Bellow's *More Die of Heartbreak*. There are more there; some of the large dictionaries even give no clues as to their meaning. The quizzes which follow are admittedly from some dictionary of difficult words although some of them are endearingly so.

989. **ANOMIE** or **ANOMY:** (a) state of conflict (b) envy (c) anarchy (d) lack of social or moral standards (e) lack of religious consciousness in a society

990. **EIDETIC:** (a) being the same (b) of visions of the distant future (c) of sharp, but imaginary images of the past (d) unquestionably true by virtue of demonstration (e) ideal or idealized

984. (d)
985. (a)
986. (a)
987. (b)
988. (e)
989. (d)
990. (c)

991. FRESHET: (a) a novice (b) a young bird (c) a new boy in a public school (d) an inexperienced soldier (e) a stream

992. CLOACA: (a) rotting matter in a stagnant pool (b) animal refuse in a slaughterhouse (c) sticky and smelly matter (d) a sewer (e) entrails of animals

993. FORFEX: (a) scissors (b) complete set of cutlery (c) forfeiture (d) quandary (e) mannerism that is foreign

994. APNOEA: (a) inability to keep food down (b) inability to breathe (c) inability to swallow (d) inability to remember (e) inability to sleep

995. MEIOSIS: (a) understatement (b) overstatement (c) obscure statement (d) easily remembered formula (e) imitative representation of nature or human behaviour

996. EPICENE: (a) monkeylike (b) a lecherous old man (c) hermaphroditic (d) young, but senile (e) a person devoted to sensual pleasures

997. CAUSERIE: (a) protective clause in an agreement (b) a short chatty essay (c) a bridge between narrow canals (d) a person who acts as a go-between (e) a highly legalized document

998. SAMIZDAT: (a) connoisseurs of art and literature (b) new wave Russian literature (c) clandestine printing and distribution of dissident writing (d) secret understanding between opposition forces (e) progressive liberalisation of economic controls

999. PLANGENT: (a) placid (b) acid (c) reverberating (d) flowing smoothly (e) beneficent

1000 FRIABLE: (a) easily destroyed (b) easily burnt (c) easily fried (d) possible (e) responsible

991. (e)
992. (d)
993. (a)
994. (b)
995. (a)
996. (c)
997. (b)
998. (c)
999. (c)
1000 (a)

VI
BONUS

Here are some more, on the baker's dozen principle — it's better to play safe when the serial numbering goes up to one thousand. We shall continue with the esoteric words, and then throw in some loan words, which may not tremendously increase your word-power, but if you care for words you wouldn't mind a little extra information about them.

B1. CARYATID: (a) fresco of nude female characters (b) fresco of clothed female characters (c) cherbs guarding doorways (d) draped female sculpture serving as a pillar (e) sculpture of angels decorating the frieze of classical architecture

B2. EKISTICS: (a) the study of sentence connectors (b) the study of animals in their natural habitat (c) the study of human settlements (d) the study of extremely backward tribes (e) the study of the pattern of suburban settlements

B3. UXOROVALENT: (a) substitute for a wife (b) slave of one's wife (c) protector of women (d) able to score only with one's wife (e) able to score only extramaritally

B4. DIASPORA: (a) dispersion (b) Utopia (c) the depths of despair (d) a gap between the teeth (e) dissonant music

B5. CRAPULOUS: (a) dysenteric (b) bogus (c) coarse (d) complaining (e) talkative

B6. ADULTERINE: (a) impure (b) woman who sleeps with somebody else's husband (c) violating action (d) illegitimate child (e) pertaining to adult preoccupations

B1. (d)
B2. (c)
B3. (d); for (e) the word is uxoravalent
B4. (a)
B5. (c)
B6. (d)

B7. EPIDEICTIC: (a) obscure (b) pertaining to meditation (c) tending to attract the opposite sex during mating season (d) exhibitable (e) in constant meditation of god

B8. FULGINOUS: (a) smelly (b) tearful (c) sooty (d) shining brightly (e) fleeting

B9. GRAVID: (a) heavy (b) juicy (c) thick (d) feverish (e) pregnant

B10. HENHUSSY: (a) devoted to one's wife (b) nagging woman (c) woman who behaves like a man (d) woman devoted to her husband (e) husband who does the housework

B11. AXIOLOGY: (a) mathematical logic (b) a system of universal law (c) study of the motion of wheels (d) theory of value judgements (e) branch of philosophy dealing with the ultimate cause

B12. HECATOMB: (a) grave of a saint (b) grave of executed felon (c) mass slaughter (d) cave of a hermit (e) grave of mass burial

B13. PSEPHOLOGY: (a) astrology (b) study of the psychology of despots (c) study of the future pattern of rainfall (d) study of deviant psychology (e) study of elections

B14. SEMPITERNAL: (a) everlasting (b) temporary (c) like a father (d) pertaining to half a day (e) happening daily

B15. SPELEOLOGY: (a) study of folk arts (b) study of folk customs (c) study of magical rites (d) study of caves (e) study of ruins

B16. STOCHASTIC: (a) of machines (b) problematical (c) conjectural (d) logical (e) serendipitious

B17. OTIOSE: (a) crude (b) obscure (c) obvious (d) sterile (e) obsolete

B7. (d)
B8. (c)
B9. (e)
B10. (e)
B11. (d)
B12. (c)
B13. (e)
B14. (a)
B15. (d)
B16. (c)
B17. (d)

B18. HYPERBOREAN: (a) inhabitant of the extreme north (b) inhabitant of the Scottish islands (c) operating at pressures higher than the normal (d) concerning Hyperion, a Titan (e) extraordinarily tiresome

B19. WAYZGOOSE: (a) busman's holiday (b) stuffed goose (c) printer's annual holiday (d) a path leading to a blocked exit (e) a stupid person attracted by easy money

B20. ZIGGURAT: (a) maze (b) winding tunnel (c) car of Lord Jagannath (d) tiered pyramidical temple (e) ancient royal chariot drawn by a hundred horses

B21. VIDELICET: (a) bridge supported by a row of piers (b) therefore (c) machine which enlarges photographic images (d) namely (e) the punctuation mark colon

B22. CARCANET (pronounced 'karkanet'): (a) a fine net of gold-thread (b) web of circumstances (c) a publisher of high class literature (d) a golden robe (e) jewelled collar

B23. PALINODE: (a) recantation (b) mournful song (c) song of praise (d) debate in verse (e) song offering to spring

B24. ARCANE: (a) stupid (b) obvious (c) long-winded (d) pedantic (e) esoteric

For the following words the English language has played the host, and often very good host, so that you wouldn't suspect the words to be borrowed from other languages, unless you were told. English has a larger number of borrowings than any other language, but that is a sign of its strength, rather than weakness. Try to identify the nativity of the following words.

B25. ALGEBRA: (a) Greek (b) Latin (c) Arabic (d) German

B26. PLUNDER: (a) Arabic (b) Persian (c) Dutch (d) German

B18. (a)
B19. (c)
B20. (d)
B21. (d)
B22. (e)
B23. (a)
B24. (e)
B25. (c)
B26. (d)

B27. COFFEE: (a) German (b) French (c) Turkish (d) Arabic

B28. LAW: (a) French (b) Latin (c) Danish (d) Arabic

B29. LOGIC: (a) German (b) Latin (c) Greek (d) Arabic

B30. ANICUT: (a) German (b) Dutch (c) Danish (d) Tamil

B31. ALLIGATOR: (a) Mexican (b) Spanish (c) Portuguese (d) Persian

B32. ATTITUDE: (a) Spanish (b) Portuguese (c) Latin (d) French

B33. CIGAR: (a) Spanish (b) Turkish (c) Malay (d) Dutch

B34. MUTTON: (a) Arabic (b) French (c) Persian (d) Dutch

B35. COCOA: (a) Swahili (b) Spanish (c) Portuguese (d) German

B36. CARAVAN: (a) Arabic (b) Persian (c) Chinese (d) Turkish

B37. QUARTZ: (a) German (b) Mexican (c) Spanish (d) Burmese

B38. YOGHURT or YOGURT: (a) Spanish (b) French (c) Danish (d) Turkish

B39. NEGRO: (a) Spanish (b) Italian (c) Latin (d) Portuguese

B40. QUIZ: (a) Unknown (b) German (c) Dutch (d) Yiddish

B41. YACHT: (a) French (b) Dutch (c) Norwegian (d) Finnish

B42. TEA: (a) Chinese (b) Russian (c) Bodo (d) Japanese

B43. STACCATO: (a) German (b) Dutch (c) Italian (d) Spanish

B44. LITCHI or LYCHEE: (a) Sanskrit (b) Chinese (c) Sinhalese (d) French

B45. PROGRAMME: (a) German (b) French (c) Danish (d) Dutch

B27. (c)
B28. (c)
B29. (c)
B30. (d)
B31. (b)
B32. (a)
B33. (a)
B34. (b)
B35. (c)
B36. (b)
B37. (a)
B38. (d)
B39. (a)
B40. (a)
B41. (b)
B42. (a)
B43. (c)
B44. (b)
B45. (b)

B46. MONKEY: (a) German (b) Portuguese (c) Afrikaans (d) Burmese

B47. HUSBAND: (a) Dutch (b) Afrikaans (c) Danish (d) German

B48. POTATO: (a) Peruvian (b) Mexican (c) American Indian (d) Spanish

B49. JACARANDA: (a) Spanish (b) Portuguese (c) French (d) Arabic

B50. SNOOPY: (a) French (b) Spanish (c) Dutch (d) Malay

B51. KINDERGARTEN: (a) Danish (b) Dutch (c) German (d) Afrikaans

B52. CHEESE: (a) French (b) Dutch (c) Latin (d) Persian

B53. BOTTLE: (a) Persian (b) Spanish (c) French (d) Portuguese

B54. KETCHUP: (a) Mexican (b) Malay (c) Modern American (d) Spanish

B55. BUTTER: (a) French (b) Arabic (c) Latin (d) Unknown

B56. BAMBOO: (a) Malay (b) Tamil (c) Burmese (d) Chinese

B57. RICKSHAW: (a) Chinese (b) Japanese (c) Hindi (d) Thai

B58. SKIPPER: (a) Dutch (b) Danish (c) Spanish (d) Portuguese

B59. CHOCOLATE: (a) French (b) Swahili (c) Turkish (d) Mexican

B60. FANCY: (a) French (b) Greek (c) Italian (d) Persian

B61. SONNET: (a) French (b) Portuguese (c) Spanish (d) Italian

B62. TAX: (a) French (b) Dutch (c) German (d) Turkish

B63. KUDOS: (a) Unknown (b) Greek (c) Dutch (d) German

B64. BALCONY: (a) Italian (b) Spanish (c) Mexican (d) French

149

B46. (a)
B47. (c)
B48. (d)
B49. (b)
B50. (c)
B51. (c)
B52. (c)
B53. (c)
B54. (b)
B55. (c)
B56. (a)
B57. (b)
B58. (a)
B59. (d)
B60. (b)
B61. (d)
B62. (a)
B63. (b)
B64. (a)

B65. ZERO: (a) Sanskrit (b) Persian (c) Spanish (d) Arabic

B66. GINGHAM: (a) Malay (b) Turkish (c) Persian (d) Sinhalese

B67. PRIMA DONNA: (a) French (b) Italian (c) German (d) Spanish

B68. OUTLAW: (a) French (b) Danish (c) Dutch (d) Spanish

B69. AMBER: (a) Arabic (b) Persian (c) Sanskrit (d) Burmese

B70. TIGER: (a) Persian (b) Urdu (c) Greek (d) Hindi

B71. TOMATO: (a) Spanish (b) Mexican (c) American Indian (d) Portuguese

B72. VERANDAH: (a) Spanish (b) Malay (c) Portuguese (d) Tamil

B73. HORDE: (a) German (b) Portuguese (c) Turkish (d) Persian

B74. SHAWL: (a) Hindi (b) Persian (c) Arabic (d) Spanish

B75. LANDSCAPE: (a) Dutch (b) Swedish (c) Russian (d) Portuguese

B76. FACE: (a) German (b) Spanish (c) Italian (d) French

B77. CHUTZPAH (meaning 'audacity'): (a) Russian (b) German (c) Yiddish (d) Hebrew

B65. (d)
B66. (a)
B67. (b)
B68. (b)
B69. (a)
B70. (c)
B71. (b)
B72. (c)
B73. (c)
B74. (c)
B75. (a)
B76. (d)
B77. (c)